JINN

USA TODAY BESTSELLING AUTHOR

JESSICA CAGE

To my father, though you aren't here with me now,
I know that you watch over me.
I love you, for as long as the sun rises to kiss the sky,
and for an eternity after it fades.

MORE BOOKS BY JESSICA CAGE

NOTE FROM THE AUTHOR

Thank you for picking up a copy of *Jinn*, the first book of the Immortalem Series. I know you're going to love it! As a show of my gratitude, and excitement to have you as a reader, I have a special gift waiting at the end of this book!

Happy Reading!
Jessica Cage

PROLOGUE

"I wish for you to be free!"

At the time, those were the sweetest words he'd ever heard. A wish for his freedom granted his release from the prison of the bottle. Freedom was the only thing he'd desired since the moment he was sentenced to inhabit the vessel. Freedom was the only thing that mattered.

Each time a new human claimed the vessel, he hoped they would use their wish to free him. That hope died quickly. People were selfish and greedy. When their luck had run out and the vessel was inevitably lost, the djinn was sent back to the bottle until another soul deemed worthy should find it. They were all so selfish—get their wishes and then they were done, off to live their lives with whatever riches they'd inevitably asked for. It was the same each time. Wish for love, wish for money, wish for power. That was what humans desired.

Aladdin died, and with his last breath, like all human possessions, the djinn was passed on. After years of sitting on the mantel, untouched, his vessel was given to a woman. Princess Batool, Aladdin's widow, gave the vessel away to her handmaiden on her deathbed. A gift for years of faithful service. When he first laid eyes upon her sad face, he thought she would want to rid herself of a life a poverty. He was ready to grant her wishes of gold, castles, and love. She surprised him, though. She was unselfish, and she saw just how miserable the djinn was in his life. They became friends. She took the time to get to know him; no one else had ever done that. He told her of his life, before he was turned into a djinn by a powerful warlock out for blood. She loved him for more than just the wishes he could grant her. Neither of them believed that the wish would work, though he'd hoped for someone to try for longer than he could remember he never knew if the act would work. It did. Her wish granted him freedom from his servitude.

He stayed with her, on her modest farm, in her modest life. She did eventually find love. She was young when Batool died and had many years of good life left ahead of her. She had four children, one of which died from an illness she wouldn't have him take away.

She knew what magic meant, what that type of power did to the person who was unlucky enough to obtain it and to the people who benefited from it. She refused to risk putting that burden on any of the people she loved. She told him God had a plan for her child, and she would not interfere. Jinn was her friend, she wanted nothing more than his comfort in a time of need. When she died, he lost the last companion he had left in life, but because of his time with her, he was left with hope that the world he knew could be a better place.

Now, the world was at war. An all-out battle between the magical beings that dwelled in the darkness for so long. The human population had been diminished to nothing more than slaves as those who grew tired of hiding their existences rose to power.

The world was a different place now, and he a different man.

CHAPTER
ONE

"When are you going to join us, Jinn?" Memories of a time long since forgotten by the world, were interrupted by the voice of a man he begrudgingly called friend. A fresh pair of beers had just touched the bar, left behind by a curvy woman who winked at Jinn and frowned at his friend. She tossed the long locks of red over her shoulder and sauntered over to the other side of the bar.

"I told you, I'm not a part of this." Jinn put the bottle to his lips and took a swig. The cool liquid was the refreshment he needed after traveling through the heat to meet his friend. He watched the bold woman who tended the bar. Every so often her eyes would dart to him and then away to something he knew wasn't holding her attention. She recognized him. He could tell by the way she looked at him. There weren't many places he could go without getting that look. He was unaligned, Switzerland in a world engulfed by war and hatred. This meant no one would mess with him, but no one trusted him either. The risk simply wasn't worth it. If someone were to discover that he was aligned with someone more powerful and they messed with him… well, that would be a risk to their lives that was not worth taking. Not to mention that he was in fact a djinn, powerful, and no longer bound to a vessel. He required no wishes to make his magic work.

"How can you continue to say that you aren't a part of it? Man, you were the start of this! Can't you see that?" Mike shook his head and focused on his breathing. He needed to calm down. When he got too excited, his words would stretch syllables in what most would find to be an unnatural way. The subtle hissing was a characteristic he tried to mask when not at home. Better chances of blending into the world around him when he wasn't hissing at the end of every sentence. This wasn't the first time he tried to convince the man to align with his side, and it wouldn't be the last. Jinn never had the guts to tell him, if he wanted to pick a team, a band of outcast shifters wouldn't be his first bet.

"How was I the start of all of this shit?" Jinn placed his beer on the table and turned in his seat to give his company his full attention. He heard the bartender sigh as his arm braced his weight on the bar and the leather jacket he wore tightened around his muscles.

"Come on, the first djinn to ever be set free, to live amongst the humans. Everyone knew who and what you were! Did you think no one else would see that and want that kind of freedom for themselves? I swear, that wish, the one that got you out of that bottle for good, that was the catalyst for everything that is happening now." Mike leaned back in his seat. "Say what you want, but yeah, you're patient zero."

"You're seriously going to sit here, drinking the beer I paid for, and try to blame this mess on me?" The world was a bleak place and someone making a wish to right a wrong wasn't the cause of it. People, both human and not, were greedy and selfish. They would do whatever it took to get what they wanted. His getting out of the bottle had no impact on that.

"Hey, I'm not blaming you. Hell, if anything we should all be thanking you. Now we're on top and the humans bow to us. They run and flee, as it always should have been!" The man laughed and slammed his empty bottle on the bar, signaling the waitress to bring another.

"This is the world you wanted?" Jinn chuckled. "I think you've had too much to drink, buddy." They'd had more conversations about the topic than he could count, and each time the discussion ended the same, with Mike complaining about how the world was a shitty place and they needed to make a change.

"Hell, it's better than the one I had before. The one I spent crawling around sewers, hiding myself in the night, and never knowing what a good life above ground was! Now I'm free to do as I please!" He stretched his arms out and winked at the woman who handed him another beer before quickly getting out of his reach.

"You still live in the shadows, Mike. Let's be real, the only difference is now you're hiding from something much more terrifying than humans." What he said was the truth. No, the slithers—shifters who turned into snakes and other reptilian creatures—weren't banned to the sewers anymore, but they weren't exactly accepted into society either. Their bodies, though bipedal and human like, were covered in scales. Some had green tones, others, like Mike, were more fortunate. He could almost pass for normal if you didn't look too closely at him. In a dark bar, after a few drinks, no one could see the difference. His ability to blend in with the grungy bar scene made their little meetings a lot easier to accomplish.

"Hiding? Me? No. Hell, I'm right here, aren't I?" He smiled as he lifted his fourth beer to his lips.

"Yes, you are… in a hole in the wall bar in the middle of nowhere, that you chose. How about next time we do this, we meet at RJ's?" He challenged him with the name of a popular bar in the inner city. Both knew that Mike would never make it past the outer rim before he was caught and either given the boot or put in jail, depending on which of the fairy patrol found him.

"Look, that's beside the point. We're getting off topic. When are you going to join the cause?" Mike pushed the beer bottle around the bar top. He was nearing his limit and needed to keep his wits for the conversation.

"The only cause I have is my own. Hate to burst your bubble, but that would mean I'm all joined up." Jinn smacked his friend on the shoulder. "I'm pretty sure this alliance thing is a one membership at a time kind of deal."

"You know, partnering with us would actually help you with that." Mike gave him the same look he'd given him whenever they played spades together—it was a look that said he had an ace up his sleeve and wasn't afraid to use it.

"How exactly would joining a bunch of outcasts and rebels be able to help me?" He launched the low blow, knowing what he said would piss Mike off, but was surprised to find he kept his cool, nodded his head, and smiled. Yeah, he had a one two punch coming.

"Us outcasts, we know a lot about what goes on inside the hives. Each one of these new bordered lands that we aren't allowed to cross into, we were once a part of them. Hell, some of us still are. Everyone has their dirty little secrets and some of them are covered in scales. We have inside info, floor plans. Secret passages. You scratch our back, and well, we'll return the favor." He pulled an envelope from the pocket of his worn jacket and slid it across the bar to Jinn. "Trust me, what's inside here will make you change your mind."

"Yeah, no thanks," he said without looking at the envelope, and got up to leave. "Besides, I'm not on the shit list with you, I can go in and out of wherever I damn well please."

"You and I both know that that is far from the truth. No one is out to get you, but not everyone is welcoming you with open arms." Mike laid his hand on the shoulder of the fleeing man, stopping his exit. When Jinn turned to him, he picked up the envelope from the bar and shoved it in his hand. "Take it." Jinn looked at his friend and chose to humor him. He placed the envelope in his pocket, shook his head, and turned to walk away. "One of these days you're going to take me up on my offer!" Mike shouted after him as he pushed his way out of the heavy bar door.

His prized possession, an Indian Chief Dark Horse motorcycle done in onyx with accents in ice blue, roared as he pulled away from the bar, leaving behind Mike and all the peering eyes. The tires kicked up the dirt into the face of the man who waved and gazed longingly at the bike he'd never be able to lay a hand on—it was an unwritten rule. Being one of the last ones ever made, the classic was something most envied. Good thing they had the smarts to fear the owner.

As he drove away, he thought of the man who handed him the envelope in his pocket. Mike was a friend, regardless of his status in life, even if the rest of the world said that he was the scum of the earth. They'd met years ago, when the first of the wars with the humans began. Mike was seconds from death, and there was a nuclear bomb headed their way. Jinn couldn't help himself, he saved the man who, when they first met, told him that they would be friends for a very long time. If he'd known then what that really meant, he might have reconsidered his actions.

CHAPTER
TWO

The world was an ugly place. When the supernatural world revealed, everyone knew the shit was going to hit the fan, and it did… repeatedly. As it became clear that the human population wasn't just going to share their world with these new creatures, everyone realized that there was only one way for things to go. War.

The humans tried their best to fight back, resulting in nuclear warfare that destroyed much of the habitable lands. People like Mike, his snake-like friend, stayed far from civilization for fear of being either exposed to those they betrayed, or caught in the crossfires of another disagreement. They'd learned that the outskirts, those lands deemed unfit for even the most trivial version of a quality life, were their safest place to dwell.

Jinn, not wanting to be confused with siding with the fairies of the inner city, stayed just before the outskirts. Far enough from the general population, but not so far that he couldn't enjoy the finer things in life. He had no enemies, but he wasn't exactly flush with friends either. There were few, those he collected along the way, but most died, either casualties of war or simply old age. Not all died, some simply betrayed him, wanting nothing more than to use him for his power. Because of one too many betrayals, he learned to keep to himself.

For a long time, he created his own paradise. After roaming the earth, encountering some of the worst people he could imagine, he retreated, and gave up on the hope for a better world. He didn't want to be around humans, those who wanted nothing more than to have him grant their wishes. No longer able to force him to do their will, they resorted to bargaining, bribery, and some of the lowest forms of trading he'd ever heard of.

In time their greed and malice made him sick to his stomach. To escape this, Jinn crafted a world all his own. His world existed in a bubble of space just beyond the reaches of the Earth and was a simple place that made him happy because of its familiarity. A farm where cows roamed, grazing on grass that grew abundantly. There were animals of all sorts, innocent, only taking what they needed to survive, never more. Each morning he woke up to a beautiful sunrise, and each night he fell asleep watching the moon kiss the sky and hearing the hum of the woman he loved. She wasn't with him, but the memory of her voice would never fade from his mind.

It was easy to hide, but in time he became bored with the things his magic created. He wanted companionship, outside of animals who were less than great for stimulating conversations. The memory of the voice that once brought him comfort became something to haunt him. Each time, he felt guilt, anger, shame, for what happened to her. He tortured himself with the echoes of her for far too long and eventually realized that if he didn't leave his designed world, he would lose his mind.

When he returned to Earth, back to reality, so much had changed. To him he'd been gone for just a few years, but the reality was that he'd been away for much longer, centuries in fact. Gone was the time of corsets, and men in white wigs. The women wore less fabric than he could fathom, and the men were just as… expressive with their appearances. He came out of his shell just in time to see the world go to hell in a handbasket.

It was the 80's. He'd missed the times of discos, he kicked himself for that, and the 40's. If there was ever a time for a djinn to shine, those were the days. He read up on all that he could and brought himself up to date on all the wonderful and horrific things he had missed out on. So much life had passed. The world had taken leaps toward technology, and he could see that happening more and more as time passed.

There was a different energy to the world. The energy he felt was strange and yet familiar and in time he would understand that what he felt was the restless spirits of those in the supernatural world. They were all still in hiding, lurking in the shadow, being sure not to be discovered, but an uprising was coming. He could sense the rebellion in the air. Another thirty years had passed before the first exposure, thirty years before their world would be revealed to the humans. Fifty years after that they would take over, following a twenty-year war. For the first time in the history of their kind the human population fought together. They put aside their petty differences to face a common goal. Their forced union was poetic in the obvious way. Tragically beautiful how they would band together in the end. Jinn had no idea how far things would go or how ugly things would get once they'd crossed that line... no one did.

Though he was back, with the way things were, he decided to keep a low profile. Odds were that no one would recognize him, but there were immortals, a few he'd run into before he slipped away to his own paradise. They would know him. If they were still around, there was no doubt that they would come for him if they found out he'd come out of hiding. He thought about changing his appearance, but he liked the way he looked. How could he take away from his six-foot four-inch broad frame? How could he fathom diminishing the muscles, or fading out the melanin in his skin?

His appearance was the last thing that kept him grounded—looking in the mirror and seeing the face of a man who wanted nothing more than a good, simple life. The face that reflected back in the mirror reminded him of who he really was, not the person they wanted him to be. Instead of the tall afro of reddish curls he once had, he sported a low cut that paired well with the full beard at his face. He'd later grow his hair back out, missing the length of it, but at the time the close cut helped him blend in a bit better.

His first encounter after returning, was with an older human woman named Claire. He remembered her well—light skin, dark hair, and a smile that brought him back to his childhood. She looked so much like his mother, he nearly asked her if she knew who her ancestors were. Perhaps there was some relation between the two of them. She'd sat next to him on a park bench, overlooking a small man-made pond. He was contemplating the world, and what place he would assume in the order of things now that he had returned. He looked over to find her smiling face, eyes focused on the ducks dancing across the surface of the pond.

"You look lost, young man," she spoke to him when he continued to watch her and not speak.

"The world, it's so different now." He sighed, taking his eyes from her, and joining her in watching the family of ducks.

"Different, from what exactly?" The wrinkles of age and wisdom stretched around her grin. "World's been the same as long as I've known it. Different faces, different people running the show, but it's all the same."

"I remember the world being so much quieter than this, simpler." Jinn's nostalgic expression confused the woman for a moment but then recognition flashed in her eyes.

"You one of them?" She squinted her eyes, studying his face, and shook her head. "You don't seem like a vampire."

"Vampire?" Her blunt delivery shocked him. She spoke the word as fact, not fiction, as if it was a common topic of conversation. One that she was well versed in.

"Yeah, blood suckers. They're all around here. Reason why I have a daily dose of vervain and garlic smoothie." She laughed. "Bite me if you wanna, and you're going to burn!"

"Sounds delicious." He chuckled, knowing very well the concoction couldn't have been a palatable one.

"Tastes more like cat piss but keeps me safe from those bloodsuckers. Works like a repellent. They can smell the stuff on me, and they steer away. You, I don't know what you are, but you aren't a vampire. Your soul is quieter, your spirit less frantic."

"How do you know so much about this?" This was a time when beings such as vampires kept their existence hidden, and yet she not only knew of them, but how to avoid them at all costs.

"I grew up in a place where this world, this quiet, peaceful place, isn't all it seems to be. I escaped, years ago, but others were not so lucky. Trust me, I know that this world is not what any of us choose to think it is. For now, everyone gets to go on about their lives, not knowing all those creatures they read about in their fantasy novels are real. That the accounts are more like their history. Who do you think penned those stories? They belong to them. Their way of coming from the dark, even if the world thinks it's just for entertainment. Soon, and I hope like hell that I am long gone when that time comes, but those creatures will come to light, and this world will be an entirely different place."

CHAPTER
THREE

The old woman was correct in her assessment. He checked in on her often, though he wasn't sure why. Perhaps it was the resemblance to his mother or that she was so aware of all the things he felt she shouldn't know. She passed away shortly before the first exposure. The year was 2017. A battle in Chicago, between gods and supernatural beings, was the one that tore through the city and blew their cover wide open.

The world watched the entire event live via social media and news coverage; there was no way to contain it. While some worked to attempt to cover things up, others knew that there was no hope in trying to make the entire world forget about dragons, shifters, and a hole to another world ripping into the night sky. Those who sought control, quickly mobilized and the war was on. The ones who everyone thought were less likely to take part were the ones who changed the game. The fairies. Everyone thought them gentle creatures who would watch from the sidelines, and that is precisely why their strike was so deadly. Their uprising was swift, precise, and left the southern half of the United States in flames.

The vampires fled, taking hold of Canada. The wolves staked their claim in Mexico, but would eventually migrate down to what was once Argentina as the shifter alliances were made, and every other species did what they could to claim a bit of territory for themselves. The frenzy spread like wildfire, across the globe, and territories were fought over often resulting in entire races being homeless. The dragons took over Australia, their hub being on the neighboring New Zealand. This was before all birds of fire, the Phoenix people, were called to return to their realm away from Earth. They had no stake in the game and wouldn't be joining any alliances.

All the nations, once claimed by human rule, had been transformed. Some were ruled by monsters who enslaved the humans who remained on their lands. Others by saints who chose to live in peace. Their homes were strong, and they provided safety. The fairies were the widest spread. They had hubs across the globe where humans could find safety, if they lived by a strict set of rules. They had to stay within certain areas and were not allowed to mix with the general population unless for work. Their homes were theirs;

the fairies made no point to control what they did within their areas as long as things remained peaceful. For the most part, humans were okay with this. They were great accommodations in the face of the alternatives—living as slaves, being eaten, or becoming the subject matter for magical experiments.

Because of their ingenuity and their strength, the fairies quickly became the governing group. If things got messy, they were the enforcers of the new laws. Of course, there were those who disputed this claim, but they weren't strong enough to challenge them. As it were, the fairies were top dog and most of the world was okay with that.

Through the entire ordeal, Jinn stayed on his own. When war came knocking, he packed up and moved. For him, safety could always be found with the fairies, though he tried to stay clear of even them. When things got hairy, that is where he went. There weren't many djinns still around, and those who were, were still pawns, bound to vessels, having to grant wishes to whoever possessed them. He'd heard of an old friend, who was being passed back and forth between the gnomes. Granting wishes that kept them safe. Yeah, he wasn't in any shit, but his life was a series of wishes that provided cover for them whenever their sticky fingers brought monsters banging on their door. He would forever be their slave.

"Jinn!" The cheerful voice met him as he walked through the door of his modest home. "Back from another secret rendezvous, I see. You know, one of these days you're going to have to tell me who the lucky lady is." Praia waited for him at the door outside his home and watched him closely as he parked the bike in the garage. In the suburban neighborhood that had seen better days, Jinn claimed a mediocre house as his own. He didn't need much; he'd had paradise before, and all that did was teach him that all the lavish possessions in the world could do nothing to really make him happy. He enjoyed a simpler life.

"I know you!" The short girl bound up to the large man whose hair had grown to a shoulder length, with a large grin and eyes that examined every inch of the man in front of her.

"Excuse me?" Jinn stared down at the young girl who wore pigtails wrapped in twine, denim shorts, and an oversized shirt that hung from one shoulder, leaving the tanned flesh exposed. She held an ice cream cone in her hand and continued to enjoy the swirl of vanilla and chocolate as she watched him.

"I know who you are! I've learned about you." She licked the melted ice cream from her fingers and smiled.

"I'm sorry, you must have me mistaken for someone else." He turned to walk away. Clearly this young girl was confused, there was no way she knew who he really was.

"Jinn, Aladdin's djinn, the only one who is free!" She paused as if questioning her own information—perhaps she was wrong, but she shook that thought away. She was sure of her conclusion.

He turned back to her, quickly hushing her words. "Look, I told you, you have the wrong person! Now, move along and enjoy your ice cream."

"I'm sorry," the girl hurried to correct the offense. "I thought you were him. I, they told us, you look like him, the pictures. That would have been so amazing if you were. I'm sorry." With sorrowful eyes flooding with tears, she turned from him.

"Wait!" Dammit, she had to cry, and Jinn was never one to allow a girl to cry.

"I said I was sorry," she pouted with full tears sliding down her face, and wide eyes full of apology. He could have turned away, allowed her to think she'd made a mistake. She would get over it eventually.

"No, okay, you're right." Though he told himself he would never reveal his identity, there was something about her that made him trust her. It could have been her innocence, her obvious reverence for life, or just the feeling of being recognized by someone who he could already see wanted nothing from him. Or, it was because he was a big ol' softy and she had pulled at his heart strings. Either way, he believed that the girl was curious, not wanting, and that made him want to know her. She followed him around for the rest of the day, asking questions about his life and where he'd been. When the sun left the sky, she asked if she could see him again. She wanted them to be friends and promised that she would never tell anyone else about him. He'd given her a way to communicate with him, a charm she wore around her neck. When the war started, that connection was how they stayed safe, delivered messages without others knowing. She was the only person he trusted without pause.

⁂

"Glad to see you here again, Praia." Praia was a fae, who were not to be confused with the fairies who ruled. Make that mistake and you might lose your tongue. Literally. It wasn't a hard error to make considering they were cousins and shared most of the same physical attributes.

Praia's people, though strong, kept a discreet life. This has always been their way. They were powerful, but once their king announced that his people would not fight for the right to rule, they were left alone. To rule would mean to allow the world to see inside their homes and this was not what they wanted. The lands which had always belonged to their people were the only ones untouched by fire.

"Why would I ever tell you who she is? So you can bite her head off?"

"Little ol' me? I would never do such a thing!" The woman

laughed. Praia was fit, a warrior trained to fight, as they all were. She was short, less than five feet tall, but her size was her best weapon, often underestimated because of it. Most fae were tall, slender, yet strong. Despite the anomaly of her physique, Praia was a weapon like no other. They were friends before the world changed; she was one of the few people that Jinn had allowed into his world. He met her in the 90's. She was just a kid then, out in the world, away from her home for the first time, when she stumbled across a man who felt familiar to her. She was the first to recognize him for who he really was. She saw the power in him.

"Oh yes, I forgot, you're just a sprite of a thing, so innocent." He unlocked the door and entered the house with Praia bouncing in behind him.

"Exactly, and don't you forget it!" Once inside, she did as always. She pounced on the couch, claiming the entire space for herself even though, head to toe, she still didn't take up the full length of the sofa. "So, what's for dinner?"

"Whatever your heart desires." He waved his fingers as he moved through his home, completing the series of tasks that had become habit for him. Turn on the light, switch on the filtration for air—the air outside got to higher levels of toxicity at night, being so close to the wastelands, he had to take further precautions. He then turned on the camera system which allowed him to view the inside of his garage where his baby waited for him.

"Hmm. My heart desires steak!" She grinned widely.

"Again?" He laughed. "I should have never introduced you to the stuff. Should have kept you on that veggie diet." One juicy steak conjured and cooked to perfection and the girl was an addict.

"Oh, but now I know the joys of meat!" She laughed maniacally. "Besides, I can only get steak with you. The stuff barely exists in the world now."

"Yes, how unfortunate. I guess I could conjure up a piece for you." Steak, beef in general, once in abundance, had become a rare commodity. Cows, like many other animals, were nearly extinct. They'd become a spectacle people paid to see in zoos. Of course, there was substitutions available, beef-like products for general consumption, but the conjured meat paled in comparison to the real thing.

"See, you do love me!" She sat up and clapped her hands, eager for the food he'd make.

"Like no other!" He headed to the kitchen and his little friend pulled herself from the couch to follow him. "So, tell me, what's new in the world?'

"Do you really need an update?" She reached inside of the refrigerator and grabbed a juice. "Let's see, what do I have to report? Oh, yeah, more war, more hatred. It's ugly out there. Some places are better than others."

"To think, everyone believed this world would be so much better than what existed before." He washed his hands so he could prepare the conjured meat that sat on the cutting board on the large island in the middle of the kitchen.

"Greed and thirst for power often blinds people to the truth."

"You know, you still surprise me with the things you say." Praia had always been a source for little nuggets of wisdom which Jinn enjoyed. "I wish what you were telling me was a shocking bit of information, but it's old news."

"Seems you always know everything, long before I do. I'll work on that." The woman spent much of her time, when not training for battle, in the library. Books were her world. She absorbed knowledge like a sponge, soaking up bits of information and storing them in her mind. She loved knowledge more than she loved steak.

The two ate the meal he cooked ... yes, cooked. With magic he was able to gain the meat desired, but he used his own two hands to prepare the meal. Jinn tried his best to restrain from using magic too much, because every time he did, it brought trouble to his door. Unwanted attention from people who had no good intentions. They all sought power and thought, if he could be persuaded to join them, he could give them the power they wanted so badly.

He enjoyed Praia when she visited, though lately her visits were less frequent due to the change in the climate of their new world. The climate shift told that another shift in power was coming. Everyone could all feel it. Because of this, everyone stayed as close to home as possible. Any time she left her home, it was a risk, a gamble on her life. He thanked her for her visits, but each time she departed, he begged her not to take the risk again.

When Praia left, Jinn found himself sitting on the couch, a bottle of beer in one hand, and in the other, the envelope Mike forced him to take. The blank white envelope felt like it was burning in the palm of his hand. Curiosity was nothing but the devil in disguise. His spiked interest in the secret hidden in the envelope was the true kindling to a fire he'd want to avoid. Though he knew he shouldn't open it, that the better choice was to burn the message and move on with his life, he couldn't help himself.

He broke the seal, took a swig of beer, and opened the envelope. The edge of the photo peeked out at him. *What game was Mike playing?* As he slid the photo out, he read the note written in Mike's scribble on the back of the photo. 'It's time for you to have a new cause.' When he turned the picture over, his heart stopped, and the heat that he felt in his hand raced up his arm and slammed into his chest, before it burst throughout his entire body. The deep brown of his skin became flushed with red undertones that gave his strong features a demonic look. His hair fell around his face as he inhaled a calming breath before reaching into his pocket for the phone that only held one number stored in the contacts. The line rang twice before the cocky voice, wrapped in a shit eating grin, greeted him with total understanding of why he was calling.

"I see you opened it." Mike's voice was slurred; clearly, he hung around the bar a lot longer after Jinn took his exit.

"Is this real?" If Mike was playing games, he'd chosen the wrong subject matter. Jinn couldn't promise the snake's life would continue for much longer if he found out the message he'd given him was anything but the truth.

"Do I look like the kind of guy who could make something like that up?" He laughed. "I wouldn't play with that topic anyway, man, I'm not stupid."

"She's alive?"

"Yes, Jinn, she is alive. I would never lie to you about something like this."

"How?"

"I don't know how, but what I do know, I will be happy to tell you, if you agree to at least consider joining me. This is a shitty way to do this, but I had to play the hand I was dealt, you understand."

"Meet me at the place, one hour." The angry djinn hung up the phone. Staring at the picture again, he tried to calm the rage. He needed a clear head before he headed off to see Mike. She was alive. All those years he thought she was gone. He was told she had died. All the years he'd lost with her. She was alive. Nitara.

CHAPTER
FOUR

"What is this?" Jinn held up the photo as Mike approached their usual spot, which was far away from prying eyes. Deep in the wastelands where no one ever dared venture to. Mike, and those like him, were immune to the toxins in the ground and air. Something about the ill magic that created his kind, gave them better ability to process poisons. Though they could survive there, they knew nothing else could—plants, food, everything no matter how viable, perished within moments of being introduced to the environment. Being there did nothing to Mike, except remind him that they weren't always monsters. He was born in the sewers, but his mother and father were human, turned into something else through chemical and magical experiments. Once those projects proved to have horrific results, their test subjects fled to go underground where it was safe for them.

"It's exactly what it looks like." Mike stopped just a few feet from Jinn. The wind kicked up, sending the reddish-brown dirt in the air in a cloud that would burn to breathe in. "I told you, I'm not playing any games here."

"Nitara, she's alive? Say it, tell me she is alive." He needed to hear him say it, see the words cross his thin lips. Mike was many things, but a good liar wasn't one of them.

"Yes, she is." The response was said with a straight face, not the slight uptick of the corner of his lips or the twitch of his right eye. If Nitara wasn't alive, Mike sure as hell didn't believe it to be the case.

"How?" Magic kept Jinn off the ground, and a pocket of clean air around him kept his body safe from the toxins in the air. He wasn't sure what the environment would do to him, and he wasn't eager to test out the theory. "I asked about her, to so many people. They all said she was gone, they told me she died. How is it now that she is alive?"

"It looks like that is what everyone was made to believe. Hell, it wasn't just her. As far as the world knew, there were only a couple of djinn left. According to my sources, there are more kept where she is. Tell me something … how many have you stumbled across during your time back? We all know the stories of our pasts are often twisted to better fit the message needed. Everyone knew that once you returned, you would come looking for her. While you were gone, her vessel fell into the wrong hands, and whoever had the damned thing wanted to make sure you couldn't find her. After a while she fell off the map completely. I don't think much effort was ever put into trying to find her, but when I saw the picture, I recognized the charm around her neck and knew she was your girl."

The crescent moon was Nitara's favorite. Whenever it touched the sky, she would sit for hours staring at it. Those moments were the best part of his day, watching the way she lit up as she bathed in the moonlight. He wanted to experience that every day, so he carved the moon out of a small piece of stone. The charm hung around her neck on a thin piece of leather. He noticed his gift to her in the photo but told himself that it was someone else's. Someone playing a game.

"Who?"

"Jinn—"

"Who has her, Mike?" he yelled. "Why else would you give me this? Why else would you tell me now?"

"To wake you up! You think you can just sleep through the shit that's happening here. You act like what's going on around here doesn't affect you, like you just aren't a part of the world. Now you can't deny anymore. Like I said before, you are a part of all of this."

"You knew this, all this time and you said nothing! We're

supposed to be friends, but instead of telling me that my wife is alive, you decide that the best way to tell me that my wife is alive is through blackmail. What the hell do you want from me?"

"That's not what this is. I heard rumors, whispers of her life. I had to be sure, I had to find out for myself before I brought this to you. What good would it have been to tell you before I took the time to verify the facts? Like I said, us outcasts, we hear things. We know things, but I had to verify. There was no way I could bring this to you without proof, knowing what you would do." He looked Jinn square in the eyes; they both knew that if he had been lying, the snake's head would already have been removed from his torso. Jinn was a good dude, but he had a temper, and nothing sent him over the edge like the loss of Nitara. "Look, join us, help us and we can help you get her back."

"There it is! Right there!" Jinn yelled. "I knew it, you are just like everyone else. This shit," he held up the photo, "this is your bottle, something for you to hold over my head so I can grant you a wish."

"Jinn, it's not like that."

"Yeah, right, Mike. Sure." He turned away from the man and headed off toward his bike, which waited completely covered to avoid any damage from the wastelands where they met.

"Where are you going?" Mike called out behind the djinn.

"I got some people to talk to, and if you know what's best for you, you will refrain from following me."

"Jinn!" Mike started to run after him but slid to a stop, nearly falling, when Jinn turned on him. He held his hand out and called flames that lifted from the ground. A toxic green touched the edges, the effects of the chemical in the earth. "Don't do this man!" He was surrounded, trapped by the flames until Jinn was too far out of range for him to follow.

The city of Vilar was one of the most beautiful that existed. Surrounded by lands devastated by war, the home of the fairies retained a beauty that seemed alien. The fairies used their magic to retain the life of their home through the war. None of the toxic flames that scorched the surrounding lands were able to get through their shields.

Gone were the iron structures made by men, the buildings that scraped the sky had been torn down. Every building grew from the ground, having its own pulse as life still coursed through the limbs of trees and magically reinforced vines that were woven together to craft structures of strength.

It wasn't just the buildings, or the few skyscrapers that stood tall and proud. What held the most impact was the minor things, the plants and flowers lining every path and the wildlife that roamed the streets and lived in perfect harmony with the fairies. This was the vision imagined for the world after the humans lost control. Only, Vilar was an anomaly in the new world order. Not every territory was this beautiful. Not all people had it so good. A family of langur monkeys swung above him as his bike rolled along that pathway, the engine disturbing the tranquil atmosphere as he passed.

"Are you sure you want to go there?" Praia asked, joining him after he'd parked his bike. They walked down the street headed to Vilar, the epicenter of the fairies' territory. Jinn had asked her to meet him, so he could give her an update on everything that was happening. She knew a meeting request meant he needed to vent before doing something really stupid. Never one to say no to the man who conjured her steaks, she agreed. "Nothing good can come of this."

"If they have the information I need, then yeah, I'm sure." As usual, every person they passed looked at them with questioning gazes. It was no secret that Praia was friends with Jinn, but the two of them weren't often seen together in public. Hell, it wasn't often that Praia was seen amongst the fairies at all, and Jinn ... well, he was nothing more than an apparition.

"What exactly are you willing to give them in return? These aren't the same fairies you may remember; they've changed. You know that. Anything you request from them, they are going to want a trade, they're going to want to bargain with you. You gotta think about that, Jinn." The short fae struggled to keep up with his long strides but succeeded in not falling behind.

"Yes, I'm well aware. I also know that they lied to me. In exchange for my help they were supposed to provide validation of what happened to Nitara. They were the ones who told me she had passed." He marched forward as he spoke, his temper rising. "They were the ones who fed me false information! All these years, she has been out there, and I haven't been looking for her. She is trapped in a cage somewhere and I just allowed it! I held up my end of the bargain, it's time that they did."

"I'm just saying, you may want to rethink things, sleep on it for a bit." Praia skid to a halt as Jinn turned on her. They stood, statues on display for the fairies to gawk at.

"Look, Praia, I didn't tell you about this so that you would feel a need to come with me. I understand if you don't want to do this, but I need you to understand that I have to go in there. You can't expect me to turn away from this. All this time, I thought she was gone, I thought she was dead. Now I find out that I was lied to. Hell, I don't even know if this photo is real." He took the picture from his pocket and held it up. "I need to do this. I have to find out, regardless of what fucked up fox trap I may be walking into right now. I have to know the truth."

"Nitara, she meant that much to you?" Yeah, she knew about Nitara, but Jinn had never spoken to her in depth about his love for the woman, or how much he would put on the line to save her. Jinn would walk through fire for his wife, and for the first time he was really allowing the world to see what his love for her meant.

He turned back toward the path that led to the city's center, pulled his hair up into a loose bun, and took a deep breath. How could he put what he felt into words so the fae, who was still in many senses still a young girl, could understand how he felt? His gaze swept over his shoulder to the short woman who waited for his explanation, the thoughts came as best as he could phrase them. "She meant more to me than the earth, the sky, and the endless universe beyond. She was my world, my air, so much so that my lungs refused to expand without her. Every fiber of my being is hers to command. If there is any chance that I get to have that back, that I get to love her and feel her life beside me, fueling my own, there is no way that I'm going to let that go."

"Wow, Jinn. I had no idea." She smiled at him, tears on the brink of her eyes. "Damn. I hope someone cares about me as much as you do for her. You know that I'm by your side."

"As long as I keep you fed with steak." He smiled and winked at his friend. He knew that she would support him, no matter how insane the cause. She always had.

"See, we have an understanding!" Her laughter trailed behind her as she hurried to keep up with him.

ट्रेट्र

"Wake up, sleepy head." Her voice was a melody he hoped to wake up to every morning for the rest of his life.

"Nitty." He spoke the nickname through the blanket of sleep that held his voice hostage. "Why are you up so early?"

"Up with the sun, you know. I never want to miss it rise." As much as she loved the moon, his wife couldn't bear to miss the sunrise. He wondered how she ever got any sleep.

"Ah, yes, the sunrise. How was it today?" He stretched his limbs, not wanting to sit up yet.

"It was beautiful, as always." Finally, she stepped into view, holding the carved stone between her fingertips. She played with the thing all the time, and to see her twist the delicate thing between her fingertips brought him joy. Their home was small, but it was theirs. He'd worked hard, with Nitara right by his side, to build a quiet life for the two of them. Not far from the village where they were raised, they operated their farm. The home, the sheds, and the shelter for the animals were all put together by their hands. Things were working out great for the newly married couple. The cows were good to them that year, producing enough milk to sell to several nearby towns.

"I should say the same about the sight before me now." He held his hand out to her, beckoning her to come near.

"You flatter me, as always." Like a magnet, she was drawn to him, her hand reaching out to him. As soon as their fingers touched, he pulled her to the bed and kissed her lips.

"I speak nothing but the truth to you. These lips could never part to deliver a lie to your ears." His full lips brushed against her ear, causing her small laugh to fill the room.

"I love you, Jinn." Her hand rested on his jaw, eyes peering into his as she drank in the love.

"Nitara, you will have my heart for as long as the sun rises to kiss the sky, and for an eternity after it fades."

"Jinn, what are you doing here?" The head of the fairy guard approached, the heels of her steel-toed boots knocking against the marble floor. She led her command with strength, and those who followed her, trusted in her entirely. Wherever she led, they would follow. She was second only to one, the queen.

"Good to see you too, Briar." Getting to the lobby of the crown of Vilar was easy enough, but if he wanted to go further, he would need permission. Unaligned or not, there were certain protocols in place that had to be considered. As she crossed the open space, four others joined her, facial expressions ranging in levels of excitement, from completely bored to nearly uncontrollable glee. That was the way of fairies—they all had their affinities, which gave them varied strengths and powers. Those connections also affected their personality. In most cases you could tell exactly what their affinity was by their appearance.

"Last time we saw each other, you said you'd never return here. Swore on it, in fact." She nodded and waved a finger at him as she recollected the last time she spoke to him. "So, I assume something extreme has happened to bring you here now." Briar was tall, nearly looking Jinn eye to eye. She had an affinity for fire and earth, and she looked to be made of stone. Her body strong, toned with muscle built through years of combat training. Her voice was deeper in tone, still feminine, but not the trill that Praia had. She had fair skin, and long hair pulled back into a neat ponytail that stretched the length of her back. Unlike most of the fairies he saw, she wore dark clothing, at all times. Never had he seen her in any of the colorful wisps of fabric that those who flanked her wore. She told him once that she was a warrior and warriors didn't wear clothing that flailed in the wind. Even her hair would be braided and pinned up in times of battle.

"You are correct in your assumption." Jinn grinned at the shorter of the fairies who stared at him. He'd never seen her before and could tell she was new to her post.

"So, tell me, what can I help you with?"

"You? Nothing. I need to see her." Jinn nodded to the top of the stairs to a set of gold doors enamored in flowers. They marked the entrance to the only elevator that gave access to the place he needed to go, the queen's chamber.

"Excuse me?" Briar looked over her shoulder at the elevator, and shook her head no. "You can't be serious, Jinn."

"This is as serious as it gets. I'm here to see Alesea." He lifted his finger to point to the golden doors again.

"That's a bold move, Jinn. Even for you." She nodded her head at the guards standing by the door. The gesture was a warning for them to be prepared should things get hairy. "Showing up here after all this time, unaligned and demanding to see the queen. What the hell makes you think you deserve something like that? What makes you think she would even see you?"

"She and I, we had a deal. A trade, my help in exchange for information. I've recently been informed that the knowledge she provided me with was flawed. I need to know, Briar, if she was aware of the error." He looked to the same guards at the door, acknowledging their presence. "You and I both know the weight that comes with the promise of the queen."

"You think she would lie to you, knowingly?" Briar squared her shoulder clearly taking offense to the accusation.

"I think she, like so many others, would stop at nothing to get what she wants. She wanted something from me, and I provided it. If I find out that it's true that she did not do the same, well, amends will need to be made." He took a slow, deliberate step toward her, ignoring tensed expressions on the faces of the other guards. "So, I ask you now, please, take me to her?"

"You know there is a procedure for this." Briar nodded to the blue-haired fairy on her right, who smiled at Jinn before walking off down the long hall leading to a secure room.

"By all means, please perform as you must, but do know that I'm not leaving here until I have a word with her." The large plush sofa in the lobby was a welcoming home for the djinn and his fae friend as they waited for the fairies to prepare for him to sit with the queen.

CHAPTER
FIVE

"Jinn, I have to say, I didn't think I'd ever see you again." The Queen of the Fairies spoke in airy tones that echoed throughout the cavernous room like whispers of ghosts. Sparkling eyes of blue watched him from the thrown sitting atop a platform coated in diamond dust. The chair itself was made of wood with accents of silver and gold, reaching up to the head where a stone, which harnessed the energy of the sun, was held.

"Considering your current position as queen, I think we both know that isn't true. You knew that I would be back." Jinn hid none of his resentment. She'd played him, and while he lived in misery, she sat on a literal throne decorated in gold.

"Briar." Alesea turned to her second. "Please, give us a moment alone." She stood from her throne and took the small steps down to meet them. Her dress flowed around her, tones of blues that mimicked the air that was her affinity.

"Are you sure?" Briar bristled. He knew that in most terms the fairy would be happy to see Jinn, but his tense body and tight jaw caused a different response from her.

"Jinn has always been a friend to us. Nothing has changed in that," Alesea reassured her. "Please, allow us some privacy for a delicate conversation."

"As you wish." Briar nodded to her crew who left the room ahead of her. She shot Alesea a reconfirming glance, and when the queen smiled at her, reassuring her that she would be okay, the head of the fairy guard turned to leave, waiting only for the fae who shot her a smirk. Praia, who had remained by Jinn's side, waited for her own look of approval before leaving ahead of Briar.

"You've returned for information?" Alesea inquired after the doors to the chamber sealed shut. She used her affinity, moving the air to create a soundproof barrier. What they were going to speak about was no one's concern but theirs. Briar wouldn't be far … hell, she may even be waiting by the door trying to listen in.

"No, not for that, I received that from you once before. What I've returned for is clarification. Understanding. Tell me, how is it that the last time I was here, you gave me information in exchange for my help, and yet now, many years later, I come to find out that what you told me was false?" He expanded his body and his voice, filling the room with his energy. Jinn wanted her to feel his anger. He wanted to see the fear in her eyes as she wondered if the pressure would be capable of suffocating her. He wanted her to fear what he was capable of. If she lied to him yet again, she would pay the consequences.

"I provided the knowledge I had." Alesea remained calm, her voice as cool as the breeze continuously swirling around her, shifting the thin fabrics of her dress.

"You provided hearsay, not knowledge! You said she was dead, taken out by the warlock while I was away." The two remained standing, mere feet separating her small frame and his dark form which continued to expand.

"And that was the truth that I had to provide."

"Really? I can hear it, you know, the flutter of your heart every time you lie to me. Please, do not continue." He stepped closer to her. "Tell me, did you verify these facts? Did you see her death personally? Did you do more than ask a few questions of those you passed in the halls?"

"What do you want, Jinn?" The queen lifted her chin, asserting her own power. If he dared to touch her, she would drop her shield and call for the guards.

"The truth." He paused. "Either you give me the truth I want, or I will spread the truth you hope none of your people ever find out about." His voice lowered as he leaned closer to her. He had her and they both knew it. "How would they take it? The knowledge that you, their queen, cut down the last."

"She was a tyrant, evil, and working with the darkest of magic! You know that I had to do what I did." Alesea took a step back from the djinn.

"I don't know that you had to do anything. Yes, all is true regarding her activities, but you killed her, Alesea, and you know as well as I do, fairies are loyal. They stick by their queen no matter what. You betrayed her, which means you betrayed them all."

"What can I do?"

"Correct the error you made. You have one day. I want to know the truth. Where is Nitara?" He turned to leave the room. "You will bring word, not one of your messengers, you. Or this city that you love so much will burn to the ground, by the hands of your own."

"You'll only implement yourself!" She called out the empty threat, her last attempt at swaying his decision.

"Yes, but unlike you, I actually possess the strength to protect myself." He pointed to the throne from which she climbed down. "You are nothing if removed from the throne. If disconnected from the source of your power, how many of them would be necessary to cut you down like you did your former queen?"

"Jinn, please."

He shushed her, holding up one finger to her. "One day, Alesea."

He left the room.

"Is everything okay?" Briar reentered the room once Jinn had made his exit.

"No, unfortunately, things are far from okay. The world is about to change, Briar." She dropped her head back to stare through the glass ceiling that gave her visage to the night sky. "Retrieve the seer, please."

☾J☽

"Jinn, it's you, isn't it?" The small, wisp-like voice came from beneath the oversized hood that cast a shadow so far down the front of her, he couldn't be sure she was really there. He was out for a stroll, minding his business, and once again he was recognized. He'd have to think of switching up his look, hiding his identity better. It would have to be something that didn't mean cutting his locks, it was becoming a signature look for him.

"You know, in hindsight, it was foolish of me to think I could keep my identity hidden without altering my appearance. Thought all the people who would recognize me would be long gone by now. It's only been a matter of months and the entire world seems to know exactly who I am." Walking through the park, enjoying the scenery, he'd realized he was being followed. Seven blocks with his new shadow and he could no longer ignore her quick heartbeat, sporadic breaths, or the way every third step landed with less surety than the ones before it. Jinn turned to the woman. She was of average height, and when she removed the hood of thin blue fabric covering her face, he saw that she was of average beauty, but had eyes that were a wintry blue.

"You haven't exactly been hiding if that was your intent. Did you think no one would question the large, mysterious man who was walking down the streets of Chicago with a fae?" She laughed as she referenced his first encounter with Praia. "You put a target on your back, one that was quickly removed, of course, when we realized who you were."

"Lucky for me, you stopped to do your research." He gave the woman another once over before continuing. "Who are you, what do you want?" He didn't like being called out on his activities or being informed that someone was watching him. Here they were in unassuming London, and she was questioning him about the activities in the windy city. "Have you followed me all the way from Chicago? I've been to quite a few places since then, have you been tailing me this entire time?"

"No, no. I didn't mean for it to seem that way. We aren't following you. In fact, no one knows that I am here today. My name is Alesea. I am Fairy." She held out her hand to shake his, an offered gesture he refused. With a nervous smile she dropped her hand back to her side.

"Obviously." It wasn't often he was approached by fairies, but he recognized the scent. They drew their power from the sun, and it left them with the smell of summer, no matter the season. That was the difference between her kind and the kind of the girl he found himself becoming attached to. The fae, though powerful, were strongest during the night—the moon the anchor to their power. "What do you want, and why are you here?"

"I need help, the kind that I believe only you can provide." She lowered her voice, stepping further into the shadow of the trees. Not a soul in the park was concerned with them or their conversation, but she felt the need to shadow her words from the joggers, playing children, and old men who sat on nearby benches feeding enthusiastic birds.

"What kind of help is that?" He leaned against the side of the tree, ready to make his bargain. If she wanted something desperately enough to come to him for aid, he would get something in return. "I'm sure there are many out there who would bend over backwards for a chance to help someone such as yourself."

"Many may be willing, yes, but capable no." She lowered her voice with shifty eyes. "I need the kind of help that can bring down a queen," she whispered as she scanned the area surrounding them.

"You want to bring down your queen? Why? I thought you fairies were loyal." If he admired nothing about the fairies, he appreciated their devotion. Almost to a fault, they would stick by their queen's side, trusting in her choices, never questioning her decisions on what was best for their people.

"I am loyal, to my people. Our queen, Ida, she has become a problem for us. She deals in dark magic. I'm afraid that her dealings will begin to affect our people." She sighed. "As you know, all of our magic is linked. If she continues to corrupt herself, I fear we won't have much longer until that corruption and darkness reaches the rest of our people. Some have already started to become sick, ill with something that we've never seen before. They don't realize that the root of what's wrong is our Queen. Even if they do, as you said, that blind loyalty will stop them from doing anything about it. That kind of damage could be irreversible." She stopped talking as another jogger passed by. When the man was out of earshot, she continued. "Once the darkness takes hold, there is no going back."

"That's a huge accusation you're just tossing out there. Do you have proof of anything that you're saying, or is this all just speculation?" Jinn stayed neutral, but when that chance arrived that he could make a deal in his own favor, he was always open to hearing the terms. Still, his conscience had to be clear. If he was to help her, he needed to know that she had proof of her claims. He needed to know that the queen was truly corrupted. Djinn or not, the guy had morals!

"If I can get you the proof you need, will you help me?" She looked at him with hopeful eyes.

"In exchange," the mischievous grin spread across his face. He had her right where he wanted her. "There has to be something in this for me, after all."

"Yes, of course. Anything that I can do, I'm willing. I'll do whatever I need to in order to protect my people." The woman had sincerity in her voice and her eyes. She meant it, her people were important enough for her to come and make a deal with a man once described as an extension of the devil himself.

"All I ask for is a bit of information." He looked out at the scene in the park where life unassuming, played out in front of him. "Since my return, I have been looking for someone. Someone I have not yet found. I need to know where she is. You will find her for me." His request seemed simple enough, but considering who he was, and that with all his power, he had been unsuccessful, the request was in fact a daunting demand.

"She? Who?" Alesea looked at him with a confused expression that irritated the djinn.

"My wife, Nitara." His response was a frustrated grunt.

"Nitara?" she scrambled for recognition of the name but found none. "I've never heard of her."

"Tell me how you know about me, but not her?"

"I'm sorry, no, I do not." She shook her head.

"Well, do your research, little fairy. Then come see me again." He turned, moving deeper into the line of trees, and vanished in a puff of smoke, with only the sound of his voice lingering. "That shouldn't be too difficult for you."

CHAPTER
SIX

"You seem pretty confident that she will give you what you want." Praia stared at him from the kitchen table of his home. They'd left Vilar just as peacefully as they arrived with a hasty escort from Briar who was only too eager to get the fae out of her home. There weren't any real problems between their kind, just a general underlying repulsion. The aversion had been contributed to the natural repulsion of the sources of their magic. The sun and the moon never possessed the sky at the same time, and when they did, they blocked one another out. Jinn often imagined that the two species felt that they would cancel each other out if they mingled, and neither wanted that to happen. He also wondered what that would be like. His mind produced an amazing display of power and destruction.

"It's easy to be confident when requesting a favor if you know the other person has no choice but to give you what you want." He dropped the plate of food in front of her. "Eat. It's getting late, you'll stay here tonight."

"Is that an order?" The corner of her lips lifted as she pulled the plate closer to her, so she could dig in.

"No, not an order, let's call this a suggestion. It's not safe, you can't travel alone." After the move he made by waltzing into Vilar, he couldn't be sure the once timid woman hadn't changed her ways since becoming queen. There was always a chance that she could be a vindictive bitch who would target Praia to get back at Jinn who, in many ways, had disrespected her in her own home.

"I'm fae, I can handle myself." She stretched her arms, flexing barely visible muscles. "Besides, the night is when I'm at my best."

"Though I'm sure that's true, I would still feel better if you stayed here for the night." Praia was strong and a worthy opponent, but if a hoard of fairies jumped her, strong or not, she would be in trouble and he couldn't have that on his head.

"Whatever you say!" She bit down into the meat and moaned. "God, I love steak!"

"Something is really wrong with you." He laughed as he sat down to his plate of grilled chicken. He was a fan of a good T-bone as well, but a guy could only have red meat so many nights in a row before continued ingestion of saturated fats made him sick to his stomach. Praia reminded him so much of his Nitara, perhaps that is why he allowed her to remain at his side. She was inquisitive, hardheaded, and could eat enough for four grown men and still look for more.

The knock at the door stopped Jinn from enjoying his own plate. The sound was foreign to his home because no one in their right mind dared to come there. His location wasn't hidden, so anyone could potentially pop up, but no one was that foolish … at least no one had been so far. He groaned, as he abandoned his plate and left the girl who was so involved in tearing into her food that she hadn't heard the interruption. Reaching the front door, he peered through the glass pane that allowed for a limited view of the outside world. When met with the irritated look of the fairy guard, he sighed and opened the door. "I told Alesea I wanted her to be the one to come."

"Yeah, well, there has been some … complications back in Vilar which require the queen's attention, so you got me. Don't get too down about it though. I am here with a gift." Briar stepped aside to reveal the small woman. She had skin the color of camel's hair, which she had draped in bright green fabrics that fell to the floor around her. In contrast to her soft skin and chosen fabric, her bright pink hair was pulled into a tight bun at the top of her head. Behind long lashes coated in pink mascara were orbs, deep, dark, and clouded by her gift.

"The seer?" Everyone knew the fairies had a seer. She was the secret to their success, how they managed to stake claim to power long before the war ever began. Seers were a rare thing; for this reason, she was never allowed to leave Vilar. Alesea must have really been in a desperate place to send her there freely and with what appeared to be only one guard. "Is there no one else here with you?" he asked as he peered around the pair, expecting to find more guards.

"Yes, apparently you want answers. Who better to provide them? To answer your other question, no. Alesea didn't want to risk you interpreting the arrival of a dozen fairies at your door as a threat." She tilted her head to the side. "Are you not going to let us in? The air out here is horrible. I assume you have a purifier."

"Jinn!" The pep of her voice never ceased to amaze him. He'd met many seers in his time, and they were all the same—sad, brooding, pained by the things they'd seen as a result of their gift. She was different. He wondered how she managed to cope with her visions.

"Sybella." As a result of saying her name, his voice adopted a cheery quality that was unlike him. Being around the seer had an inexplicable effect on him. Her energy was contagious. He'd known her before she worked with the fairies, before the war. She was an artist, her paintings were the stuff dreams were crafted from, and they hung in galleries around the world.

"It's good to see you again. It's been a long time." The shorter woman, who had been kept beautifully preserved by magic, reached up to hug him. He remembered when they first met, and she came straight out and told him what she could do, her gift. She didn't think that he would believe her. Most people wrote her chatter off as the crazy musings of an artist, but he knew better. When he told her he believed her, she smiled the brightest he would ever see from her. Sybella even offered to foresee his future, but he opted out of that. Mystery was what made living worth it. Besides, he didn't want to use her as so many had done to him. "You haven't aged a day."

"A curse as much as it is a blessing. I still get carded when I order a drink." He laughed as he returned her hug. Sybella wasn't allowed to leave her quarters, lavish as they may be, garden and pool included, there was no way she was waltzing into any bar and ordering a beer. "We will need some privacy, you and I," Sybella announced, and looked to Briar who huffed as she pulled the door shut behind her. They moved through the hall and headed for the living room, but Jinn nodded toward the exit, giving the fairy direction.

"Praia is in the kitchen eating now."

"Yes, of course." She muttered something else that he didn't catch as she left the room to join Praia in the kitchen. Once there, she made sure to call out her happiness over having lucked out on a free meal. Jinn frowned; he would be going without dinner for the night.

"I was told what you wish to see." Sybella sat on the chair positioned in the corner, a matching chair sat across from it, a small pedestal table just between the two. She looked at the empty seat and waited for him to join her. "Here I thought you would never let me peer into your future."

"It's not the future I want to see, at least not that far into it. Looking for something closer to the present. I need to find Nitara." He sat in the mirroring chair, the cushion stiff and uncomfortable; he got them as a visual piece, not to ever provide comfort.

"I offered this to you once before, and yet you denied me. What has changed now?" Sybella had offered to help Jinn many times because she could feel his pain. Being an Empath as well as a seer, any time the two of them came into contact, she was rushed with a wave of emotions that broke her heart a thousand times over. She wanted to help her friend, but he always refused her.

"I thought, for so long, that she had perished. I couldn't imagine a life without her, a world where she didn't exist. I didn't want to see that. To see her death would mean having to accept that she was gone. Knowing with a definitive conclusion that I would never be able to see her, to touch her, or hold her in my arms. I had to hold on to something, some hope that what I was told was wrong. Somewhere along the way I lost that hope, but it has been given back to me. This time, I will do whatever I have to do. If there is a chance that she is still out there, alive, I must know. If it turns out that all of this has been some elaborate and shitty joke, well, I am ready to know that as well."

"Your hands, please, Jinn." One deep breath, and he reached

out to her. When she touched him, he could feel everything he'd been holding onto release from him and pass through the physical connection. Yes, there was hurt and anger, but there was something more, something he'd never allowed her to see before—love. The emotion had been packed away and buried beneath years of self-torture, but it was there burning just as brightly as when he had none of the self-hatred that tried to eliminate it.

"Meld your mind with mine, let my eyes see what you see. Think of who it is you wish to find. Imagine her face, her smile, the sound of her laugh, the smell of her flesh, the texture of her hair. Think of every part of her and let that bring you to her."

It wasn't hard to bring Nitara to his mind. As soon as he thought her name, her face was there as it was every day of his life. The image of her was burned into his mind, seared into his memory, and would never fade no matter how many years passed. Her smile was as bright as the sun she woke up to meet each day. Her eyes were deep brown, pools of chocolate he loved to swim in. Her skin was honey, a perfect complement to the dark cocoa that coated his own body. She had the laugh of a nerdy teenager, snort, and all, and he loved it. That snort was his championship. That hideous sound was how he knew he'd made her truly happy. He thought of every facet of her, the curve of her hip, the fullness of her ass, the small pooch that hung in front of her, proof of her healthy appetite. He would cover her stomach in kisses each night imagining the day when that pooch would hold his child. He thought of her and with each detail, his heart warmed more by the heat of their love.

Jinn inhaled sharply as his mind was taken hostage by her. The air of the room was vacuumed away, and he was mentally transported to another place. The appearance of a room, first indistinct and far off, settled into view as the fog lifted from the transfer. Eight cages lined a brick layered wall. The only light available came from candles placed in the far right, and a small barred window at the left. Each cage held someone, hunched over in various positions on the floor of their cell. There were three witches sitting in the center of the room, their eyes shut and their voices chanting a spell he recognized. It was one of entrapment. Jinn returned his attention to the cages.

They were full, each one held a hostage, a djinn, a couple of whom he recognized. The first was Mavor, a djinn who had an issue with flames; piss him off and things went up in smoke. There was Kai, a small but powerful djinn he'd run into in his days when he was still tied to his vessel. They were both protecting their masters from a threat, and without the wishes of their masters to unlock their magic, they were forced to work together to take down an extremely pissed off dragon. He would see her a few more times before he was wished free. The others, he didn't know, or couldn't tell if he did because their faces were hidden. Inside the last cage, closest to the window, the only one illuminated by another source, her skin touched by the light of the crescent moon, was Nitara. She lifted the charm that hung around her neck to her lips. As her lips pressed against the smooth stone, a single tear fell from her eye.

"She's alive. I can feel it," Jinn spoke as he watched the woman in the cage. She stared out the window as the moonlight caressed her dark flesh. She hummed a song he'd heard her sing many times before. The lullaby was one from their childhood, a story of lovers, lost to each other. The fable said they would find each other if they believed. The story was Nitara's favorite and she would sing the song to him often. She would tell him that if they were to ever find themselves separated, all they had to do was continue to believe in one another, the universe would bring them back together.

"Yes, she is," Sybella's voice whispered. "This is as close to the present as I can get, just a few hours from now."

"Why? Why was I told before that she was dead?" Jinn slammed his fists on the table between them as he was brought back to his home, away from the woman he loved. Even with tears in her eyes, she was the most beautiful sight he'd seen.

"The last seer was corrupted. The one Alesea went to after she met with you. He gave her false information. He was with the last queen; he swore his service until death, and he meant that. He knew what you were planning and hoped to change the future by providing you with the information he thought would cause you to betray Alesea. Foolish of him as no seer has ever been able to alter the course of events. We witness, report, that is all, but Ida's corruption had gotten to him and he thought he could work around the limits of his gift."

"So?" Praia's head appeared around the corner from the hall. The sound of Jinn's anger brought her to check in on them. She had to be sure that he was okay. She was his keeper, whether he liked it or not.

"It's true. She is alive." Jinn stood from his seat and wiped his face. There were no tears, just fatigue. Sharing your mind with a Seer was a draining experience. The act of standing gave him a sense of vertigo that he had to wait out.

"Who is alive?" Briar asked, mouth full of the stolen chicken, having never been informed of what was going on. Alesea kept his request a secret, only telling Sybella what he wanted of her.

"Nitara." Jinn took a step forward but paused as the dizzying effect had not worn off. "She is my wife."

"Seriously? Where?" He should have been thrilled to know that his wife was still alive, yet he looked angry and sick. Praia halted her happy bounce. "Why are you so upset? What's wrong?"

"She is being held, somewhere in a cage, a prisoner." It hurt to speak the words and bring them into reality. His love was trapped, and though she appeared physically unharmed, she was likely being tortured while he sat night after night conjuring steaks and beers.

"We have to find her," Praia said. "We can save her, from wherever she is!"

"Where would we even begin?" Briar asked, including herself

on the excursion she wasn't invited to.

Jinn removed the phone from his back pocket, took a deep breath, and redialed the last and only number used. The line rang twice before the call was answered. "Mike, get over here."

CHAPTER
SEVEN

"Again, we meet, old friend." Mike sauntered up to Jinn with a knowing grin on his face. "Perhaps we can part ways in better form this time? You know, no circles of fire, trapping me in hazardous territories."

"I see you survived your escape from the flames. Looks like you did so without so much as a singed scale." Jinn stood outside his home, wanting to start the conversation with Mike before the three women inside could chime in. He needed to clarify a few things before they went any further.

"I'm a talented guy after all." Jinn noted the cautious way Mike moved around him. Until then, the man had nothing to be concerned about when he was around the djinn, a neutral party in a world of shit. Jinn had no stake in the game. All that had suddenly changed, just as Mike wanted. "So, I take it you found the proof you needed. You know that it's true."

"Yes, Sybella, the seer," he nodded at the closed door that stood as a barrier between them and the others, "she confirmed it."

"Good, that will save us some time here." Still not sure what his old friend wanted; Mike kept a safe distance. He wasn't a fool. Jinn was a powerful being and if his ploy had pissed him off, Mike could be in danger.

"How do I know that you can really take me to her?" Jinn took the picture out of his pocket and held it up for Mike to see. "Wherever she is, I'm sure there isn't an open-door policy. What makes you think you can get me in?"

"Hey, I got the photo, didn't I?" Mike feigned a hurt expression. "Look, man, a shift is coming, power is about to change hands, we can all feel it, and I know you can too. Right now, our people have a real shit deal in the world and I'm looking to change that. I got a little girl coming, man. I'm about to be a father. I can't have her growing up out there in all this shit, not like I did."

"Tell me what you want from me. What do I have to do?" There was always something, the man didn't just want Jinn to say he would be on his side. Odds were, he wanted access to his power, how else would a djinn be of use to the slithers?

"Jinn, you're powerful as hell. I know you try to deny that. You keep your shit at bay because it will make you a target, but I know the truth, I know what you can do." Taking a chance, Mike stepped closer to the agitated man still holding the picture of his lost love. "Help us, get our people a better deal out here. I'm not asking for much, I'm not trying to rule the world. Like you said, this shit was supposed to be better, for all of us. Hell, all we ever wanted was to not have to live our lives running and hiding from humans, but look at my people, look at how we are forced to live." Mike put it all on the table. Now that he had Jinn listening, he couldn't waste the opportunity. "This isn't the life any of us deserve. Yeah, some of us are pretty bad, but that is because they are a product of their upbringing. You spend a lifetime in sewers, stealing to survive, and let me know how you make it out."

"What makes you think I can do anything?" Jinn returned the photo to his pocket. There it would remain until he saved his girl, and long after. It would serve as a reminder to never let her out of his sight again.

"That day, when you saved my life, I saw everything. I know I always told you that I didn't know what happened, but that was a lie. That bomb was coming at us, and you stopped it." Mike confessed the secret he'd kept to himself for longer than he intended to.

When the war started, they were south. Mike had just stumbled out of a bar as alarms blared all around him. The night was young, but he'd gotten an early start on drowning his sorrow. Unsteady legs carried him forward, and with a miscommunication between his brain and his feet the man went tumbling forward. A firm grip on the back of his worn-out denim jacket saved him from being roadkill. He turned to find the man he would come to be great friends with smirking at him and warning him about sobering up. Soon the streets were flooded with people, screams of terror rung out around them and Jinn released his hold on Mike. The slither fell backwards, hitting his head on the side of the building he'd just stumbled out of. As he slipped into unconsciousness, he saw it. In the sky above, it looked like a football trailed by flame—the missile was headed right for them. As the others screamed and ran with false hope of finding shelter to sustain the blast, Mike watched the djinn. With no wish at all, he held his hands to the sky. A trail of blue light shot from his palms, encapsulating the approaching missile, and turning it into the best damn light show he had ever witnessed. Jinn always said he'd simply transported them out of the danger zone, but Mike knew the truth. "If you can do that, make an entire nuclear weapon implode and turn into dust, then you can help us broker a better way for our people. That's all I'm asking. We need leverage, we need some way of getting peace. I'm not even asking for you to make anything implode, no fireworks necessary, just foster a conversation for us."

"Where is the place in the photo?" He made no comment on the events of the past. "Where is she?"

"Does that mean you are going to help us?" Mike wasn't a fool, he had to get Jinn's word before he gave up any bit of information.

"Fuck!" Jinn cursed the sky, yelling out into the night, frustrated that yet again, he was being pulled into some shit that had nothing to do with him. "Yeah, I'll help." He sighed. How could he say no when denying the man his request equated to losing his only chance of getting to Nitara? There was nothing saying that he would ever get another chance. She was trapped, caged up like an animal. He couldn't leave her that way. He couldn't let them continue to do whatever they were doing to drain the light from her eyes. "I'm assuming you have a plan?"

"Of course, I do." The grin stretched across his face. "As long as I've been waiting for this moment, you think I wouldn't have a plan figured out?"

"Great. Let's hear it."

"Okay, well—" Mike started, but was cut short.

"No, not here. Follow me." They weren't in a place known to have many visitors, but Jinn knew that he was followed before and after his little visit to Vilar, he wouldn't be surprised to find out that Alesea had eyes on him again. Despite what Briar said, the queen was no fool. "As far as I know, we're being watched right now. Let's take this conversation inside."

2

Jinn had never invited Mike to his place before. This wasn't because he didn't want him there, but his home was too close to Vilar. If Mike was ever seen there, the discovery would be a problem for them both. Considering he'd taken the plunge and decided to join up with Mike, he no longer cared about taking the risk. Hell, it wouldn't be long before everyone figured out his decision anyway. Regardless of the risk, he wasn't ready to go to Scourge where Mike's people were. He needed to be sure they were on the same page and had a solid strategy before they went any further. They needed to come up with a plan with the least amount of liability and exposure involved.

Scourge was a place of torture; living there meant dealing with the worst the world had to offer. Nuclear and magical warfare combined to change the climate of the earth, making parts of the world completely uninhabitable. Mike's people were tough, able to adapt to any environment, but it didn't mean they were happy to live in a place where plants couldn't grow, and the animals couldn't survive. They had to travel hours to get food, and even then, there weren't many places welcoming to their kind. Jinn understood Mike's plea, he got it, he just really had no desire to be involved. Decades of war and he managed to keep his head out of the mess, but now he was diving in, cannonball.

Regardless of Mike's passion to uplift his people, it was their own fault that life had dished them such a shitty meal to partake. The Slither leaders tried to play both sides of the field. They never truly settled on a side during the war. When everyone found out that the slithers were double crossing those they'd sworn allegiance to, they were cast out by all sides. Their people were pushed into the Scourge as their punishment for not being strong enough in their convictions to choose a side to fight for. Jinn had no sympathy for them. He was neutral, yeah, but he stayed out of the conflict completely. He remained committed to refusing to aid or handicap either side of the war.

"What do you want?" They stood in the garage, not yet entering the house where the three women waited. He'd used magic to cloak Mike's entrance to his home, anything to avoid anyone knowing what he was considering. If anyone was watching them, they would believe that Mike turned, and exited through the same sewer system he used upon his arrival. "Foster a conversation, what exactly does that mean?"

"It means exactly what it sounds like, Jinn. I want face time with the fairies, a chance to talk to them and get my people out of Scourge. That's all. I just want a better life for us."

"Seriously? That's all you want? I find that hard to believe, Mike."

"You're good with them, they like you, and they fear you for your power. If anyone can help us, it's you." Mike sighed. Jinn understood his frustration, but he had to make sure that Mike wasn't trying to mislead him about his true intentions. "Hell, you know damn well, no one else would be able to get them to even consider this! If they think that you have sided with us, for real, they won't have a choice but to listen to our terms."

"I'm not going to walk in there with threats, Mike."

"I'm not asking you to. That would only mean more war, and a worse outcome for my people. I just need you to be convincing enough that they hear what I have to say."

"So, I convince them to give you what you want, in exchange for what exactly?" Jinn walked over to his bike, picking up a cloth and wiping away a bit of dirt on the side. "You know just as well as I do, everything is a bargain. You're going to have to offer them something big for them to even consider this, Mike. As far as I know, you have nothing to offer."

"That's the other bit of it. They help us," he paused, the next words would likely cause a flash of blue anger, "and you help them. You're just about the only one who has a chance of keeping them from losing their shit right now."

"Losing their shit? What the hell are you talking about, Mike? What do you know?" The fairies were the most powerful entity on earth. Outside of the fae, who opted out of the nonsense from the jump, who could possibly be strong enough to take them out?

"I told you that there is a change coming, and someone very powerful has put a target on the fairies. It's all over the underground.

Whoever this dude is, he is strong as fuck, like something I've never even heard of. He has some crazy shit in the works. Bits and pieces of his plans leaked out, but the bottom line is, he is out for power and the fairies are on the chopping block. They're going to need you, man."

"Now I understand... your idea is for me to pimp myself out to them so you can get what you want?"

"Not just me. Remember Nitara." Mike leaned against the workbench as Jinn admired his bike. "It's a win all around, for everyone involved."

"I can find her on my own. I don't need you for that." He grunted as he tossed the cloth back onto a nearby bench.

"Maybe, in time, but I know exactly where she is. She is hidden, and magic can't be used to find her. By the time you work the network of misfits to get the information that will lead you to her, it will be too late."

"Too late?" Rage snapped his calm mind in half. Jinn turned on his friend, two hands planted against Mike's chest and pushed back against the bench and held him down with his back bent awkwardly over the table. "What do you know? What do you mean too late?"

"I don't think she is being held captive for the hell of it." He didn't struggle with Jinn as he pinned him down; his instincts would be telling him to fight, but Jinn knew that Mike was smarter than that. "I think there is more going on. And I think that it could just mean the end of your wife's life, and for real this time," Mike choked out. "Come on, man, let me go. I'm not here to fight. I want the same thing you do."

Jinn relaxed. "Sorry, man." He released Mike, who slowly rose, rubbing the sore spot on his back caused by a rogue screwdriver.

"Are you okay?" Jinn had returned to himself as quickly as he snapped.

"Yeah, I'm good. Let's just get this shit over with."

"We have to find out who this witch is, and where she is keeping Nitara." Praia was still actively plotting; Briar looked annoyed, but Sybella appeared amused by the fae's enthusiasm. The three women occupied the living room. Praia periodically gave the seer the side eye due to her new position on the couch. She considered telling the woman that she was in her spot but thought better of it. Being rude to the Seer of the Fairy Queen would be in poor taste.

"For the hundredth time, we need to wait until Jinn gets back before we can do any plotting or speculating." The fairy rolled her eyes. "We don't have enough information to go on. What exactly are you going to do with a three second description of a vision of a future just hours from now?"

"I can help with that." Mike stepped through the threshold and Praia hissed. Knowing exactly what he was, she was ready to defend herself and her friends. "You know, with the information bit, unless you all would prefer that I not be here."

"What the hell is he doing here?" Praia jumped back, and Briar held a similar defensive stance; neither of them trusted his kind.

"He is a friend and he's here to help me find Nitara. If it weren't for him, I wouldn't even know that she is still alive," Jinn inserted. "Praia, Briar, please settle down."

"Mike, at your service." The unwanted visitor bowed, and Briar rolled her eyes. "It is my greatest pleasure to meet two such beauties."

"I didn't sign up to be working with bottom feeders." Briar spoke to Jinn directly, refusing to acknowledge Mike, who feigned a look of hurt.

"Look, right now, Mike is the best bet I have at saving my wife. If you have a problem with working with him, the door is to your left." He nodded toward the exit. When she didn't take the offer, he continued. "I don't have the time or patience to be dealing with your petty ideas of who is or isn't good enough to fight beside. Please do not make the mistake of misunderstanding why I am here. My intent isn't to make sure you're comfortable."

"Fine." Though Briar would have loved to walk out, she was ordered by Alesea, her queen, to help Jinn in whatever way he felt necessary. If she could figure out what the hell he held over the queen's head, maybe she could use the information to bargain for some more vacation time. "What does lizard boy get out of it?"

Mike bristled at the insult, and Briar prepared for a fight; she was egging him on. The Slithers came in all sorts—lizards, snakes, those who were the result of the failed experiments were grouped together. Despite the insult from Briar, Mike kept his gaze trained on the smaller of the two women. Praia was still on edge, waiting for the tension to ease. Briar was a shit talker, but if he didn't act accordingly, he could see that Praia who was so clearly on edge, would be the one to jump first.

"Bottom line is, Mike is here to stay, so get over it," Jinn stated, new power and agitation in his voice. "Let's put the petty shit aside so we can focus on what really needs to be done, shall we?"

"Where is Nitara?" Praia asked. There was nothing more to say on the topic, but she could finally start the plotting Briar was making her put off. If Mike had information, she would extract every bit of it from him, one way or another.

"She is being held captive within the Collective. In the Ashen area," Mike answered her. "That is where my intel came from. I have friends in the area."

"Of course, you're friends with witches," Briar mumbled under her breath. Since the wars, the coven was at the top of their list of enemies.

"Wait, she is actually inside of the Collective?" Praia questioned. They'd realized magic was involved, but to have her in their territory meant that this was bigger than just a rogue witch trying to get a genie to do their bidding.

Not long after the war started, the covens were forced to take up together, realizing that apart, they would never be able to defend themselves against the fae and fairies who were a larger, more powerful force. The word was put out and covens from all over the world merged together. Their land was one of the few safe places for humans… well, certain areas, not all of the witches felt the humans deserved safe haven after the havoc they'd caused on earth. Those with the affinities for the forces of nature, who pulled their magic from the natural occurrences—air, earth, fire, and water—were less likely to befriend the human population as they blamed them for the diminished condition of the earth.

They called their area, formally Africa, the Collective. Within there were sectors, dividing the different covens and faiths. The land was split evenly and with each coven in mind, for what they would need from their land. A treaty was formed; there would be no infighting, and everyone would be able to do as they pleased within their own sectors. Ashen was the darkest area—where witches practiced dark magic, and humans were slaves or subject matters, test dummies for new spells and potions. The Ashen was no vacation spot for Mike or his people. Most of them avoided the place and for good reason. It was because of experiments such as the one practiced by those who used dark magic that he and his people were the monsters everyone saw them as.

"Yes, it's true." Mike nodded. "It's going to be hell trying to get her out of there, too. They have her deep in the area, which means trying to get in without being seen is going to be quite difficult."

"How the hell do you expect us to believe that you made it in and out of there alive?" Briar asserted. Briar, like most people had been programmed not to trust Mike or his people. They were told to always assume that the slithers were lying and hiding their true agenda.

"I never said I was in there." He flopped down on the couch, which caused Praia to bristle even more. "I said that is where my intel came from."

"Well, how did you find out that she was alive?" Briar dug in further.

"Contrary to popular belief, not everyone hates my kind. Some see that we got the short end of the stick." He sighed. "I have friends who have access to things you and I would never be able to get to."

"Yeah, well, it sounds to me like you struck up a deal with some shady people, Mike," Jinn offered, because the latter was more likely the case.

"Either way, it got me what I needed, didn't it? Look, do I need to continue to defend myself here? I got you the information, and you know now that what I provided was the truth. What more do you need? Does it really matter to you what methods I used? It's all true and sitting here debating my tactics isn't going to change fact to fiction."

"One of these days, you're going to make a deal you aren't prepared to square up on." Jinn handed Mike a beer from the bar in the corner of the room, an offer of peace. The man was right. How he came about the information didn't matter. Nitara was alive and in danger, all that Jinn was concerned with was making sure she survived.

"Yeah, well, that day has yet to come." He cracked open the beer and took a big swallow. "Besides, that's how I get by. Bargains and deals. That's the world I live in. I don't expect you to understand what that's like."

"So, we're headed to the Collective?" Praia asked. "What's the plan for getting in and out?"

"We?" Jinn shook his head. "We aren't going anywhere, you're staying here."

"Oh, come on, Jinn, I can help! When are you going to stop treating me like a child?" She pouted.

"When you stop making that ridiculous face every time you don't get your way." He laughed at the silly way she poked her lips out and made her eyes as big and low as possible to further punctuate her disappointment. "Besides, you'll need to stay with Sybella. We can't leave her without protection. Mike and Briar will come with me."

On the couch, sipping on a mint tea, Sybella smiled.

"Whoa, Jinn, man, I said I would deliver information, I never said anything about going to the Collective with you." Mike put his beer down. "I mean, that place is crazy, and it gets worse every day as far as I know."

"No, you said you would help me, and if you want me to keep my end of the bargain, you're going to gear your ass up." He turned to Briar. "Any objections from you?"

"Nope. I have my orders, as long as you require my help, I'm here." She threw her hands up in the air, a sign of defeat, then went to the bar to make her own drink. Scotch, neat. She knocked back a glass and then poured another.

"Good. Well, rest up, do whatever you need to do to get prepared. We leave in the morning." Jinn stomped out of the room and headed to his bedroom, leaving the four alone. Not long after he left, Briar was snipping at Mike, Praia was complaining to Sybella, and the stocked bar was quickly emptied of all its contents.

He drowned out the murmurs of the others with his own internal debate. Questions about his love for Nitara—would she be the same as he remembered? She looked the same in the vision, the inner light of her joy faded, but that would happen to anyone trapped in a cage and held hostage by witches. How long had she been that way? How many years did she spend chained up while he roamed free, refusing to get involved? If he had taken a side, might he have been able to save her? So many questions flooded his mind, but he knew that no amount of speculation could change what had occurred. All he could do was move forward. She was alive and he would find her.

He laid his head on the satin-covered pillow. The shower did nothing to ease his mind. There was a burning in the pit of his stomach, the searing feeling of regret, of loss, and of heartbreak. Closing his eyes, he willed himself to sleep. He needed the rest. Nitara was waiting for him.

CHAPTER
NINE

"Nitara," he whispered through the dark, his words barely audible. There wasn't time; he had barely made it to her and once the unconscious man was found, stashed in a nearby closet, they'd know he was there. He'd taken out several men on his way down to the dungeon she was kept in.

"Jinn?" She looked confused as her ears recognized the sound of a voice she hadn't heard for over two thousand years. "Is that you? Heavens, I'm going crazy." She moved to her knees and prayed for her sanity.

"Nitara, yes, it's me." He moved closer into the light so she could see him, dark skin illuminated by the soft yellow glow of candlelight.

"How?" She pulled herself back to her feet, leaning against the bars that seared her flesh, causing her to jump back. "How are you here?"

"It doesn't matter, I'm here now. I've come to get you out of here." He continued his approach and as he did, she smiled, eyes wide and grin full, but something felt off. He reached for the lock, but her eyes darted frantically from the restraints to him, causing him to pause. Something was wrong.

"What are you doing? Open it!" She pleaded for him to continue. "They will come. You have to get me out of here!"

"Nitara, are you okay?" He took a half step back as he tried to get a gauge on the woman in front of him.

"Yes, of course, my love," the desperation was heavy in her voice. "Now, just open the door, and let me free."

"Nitara…" Sweat formed on his brow. The heat in the dungeon was heavy, moist, and it gave the space the smell of sweat soaked towels after they'd been forgotten inside a gym bag for a month. He considered their situation, and the woman in front of him. As much as he wanted to let her out, something in his gut told him not to. She wasn't the woman he remembered.

"Open the door, Jinn." Her tone softened, she tried to lull him into giving her what she wanted.

"Are you sure you're okay?" Again, he questioned her, needing reassurance that he was doing the right thing.

"Open the door!" She yelled and slammed her hands against the cage, burning her flesh again. "Dammit! Let me out!"

"Nitara—"

"You have left me alone for all this time. Now you've returned only to tell me that you won't let me free. Why are you here?" She screamed as she pounded her fist against the metal bars. "I will kill you. The moment I am out of here, I will hunt you down! Do you hear me? I will make you pay for this! You did this to me!"

"I…" He backed away from the cage. She wasn't who he thought she was; she wasn't who he wanted her to be.

"Jinn!" Never had she spoken his name with such hatred, or with such contempt.

Just as he turned to walk away from her, the love who wasn't as he remembered, the lock fell away from the cage; the broken metal device clanked against the concrete floor. The door swung open with a high-pitched squeak of the hinges. He turned back just in time to see Nitara lunge for him, hands poised for his throat.

The dream shook him, as he sat up in his bed, covered in beads of sweat. Nitara, what if she didn't want him to come? What if she hated him? He wiped the sweat from his brow and lifted his hair from his neck to allow air to flow against his skin. He stood and looked at the king-sized mattress which now held a full impression of his body, outlined in sweat. He was going to need another shower.

The soft tap on the door wasn't enough to pull him from his thoughts, neither was the low whisper of his name when she entered the room. It was the warmth of her hand as she touched his arm, which snapped him into the present, moments before he nearly killed her. His vision cleared and he saw the frightened face of Praia, his large hand, dark flesh, in contrast to the pale tones of her throat.

"Praia?" He questioned if he held the fae girl he cared for, or the shrew of an ex that had just attacked him.

"Jinn, please." She pulled at his hand, but when he refused to let up, she placed her hand on his wrist and emitted a small shock, just strong enough to make him release her.

"Praia, I'm sorry, are you okay?" He stepped away from her, as a feeling of shame washed over him. For the second time in a matter of hours, he'd attacked someone he cared for.

"Yeah. I'm fine." She rubbed her throat and coughed. "What the hell was that about?"

"I'm sorry, I had a dream, it just really messed up my head." He grabbed an elastic band from the bedside table and used it to tie his hair up.

"Guilty conscience, making you dream your wife wants you dead. Could you be any more stereotypical right now?" She kept a safe distance from him. Jinn knew she cared for him, but the man did just have his hand wrapped around her throat! "That is why I came here. I had a feeling you were struggling with this. Now, had I known you would try to take my life, I would have stayed in my room."

"I didn't mean to hurt you, are you okay?" He examined her neck. There was a small bruise that would likely heal in a few hours, but he frowned knowing he'd hurt her. "Shit, are you in a lot of pain does it hurt a lot?"

"I'm fine. You wanna talk about it?" She rubbed her neck and frowned at him. "Your dream, what happened?"

"Praia, I just... it's been a long time since I saw Nitara, and this, who we are now, it's my fault." His regret was unending. "Had I listened to her; we would have lived normal lives. We would have had a family, children. We would have grown old together on our little farm, happily. I just had to get involved, I had to interfere. My refusal to stay out of things then, though I thought I was doing the right thing, is the reason that she has spent an eternity in servitude and is now locked up like an animal!"

"What do you mean? What happened?" She sat on the foot of the bed. "How is any of this your fault, Jinn?"

"We weren't always like this, Nitara and I. We were normal... well, close to it. We were witches. We left our coven at a young age, though, choosing to live simpler lives. Our coven was starting to look for power., They wanted to expand their territory. We agree that we didn't want any part in that, and it was something neither of us wanted. Instead of joining the expansion, we built our home, a dairy farm, not far from a local town. We were one of the few in the area, so things were damn good. We were happy. Nitara wanted to use our magic as little as possible, and I agreed.

I went along with what she wanted. But the nearby towns

began to be attacked by something wicked, a dark evil, I had to do something. I refused to sit by and watch as they all suffered. Nitara asked me to stay out of it, begged me to. I didn't listen.

"I thought I could save them, protect them. I had no idea what was really plaguing their lands. I'd never encountered magic so dark, or so powerful. What was more disconcerting, was the man who wielded it. There is no way he should have possessed such strength. I managed to get away and ran home, which was the biggest mistake. The asshole. I should have never returned to her. It followed me and he cursed us, making us what we are now." Jinn fell back, sitting on the edge of the king-sized host of his nightmares.

"You've been blaming yourself all this time?" She sat next to him. Jinn had calmed, and he knew that she could feel that shift. The girl had a weird way of understanding him like no one else had been able to. He was thankful for her, because she kept him grounded.

"Who else is there to blame?"

"I don't know… maybe the asshole who terrorized a village, then decided to curse you for attempting to save it?"

"She may not want to see me. She may not love me anymore."

"Yeah, that's a definite possibility, but we both know that it's not going to stop you from going over there, kicking some witch ass, and doing whatever the hell you have to do to save her. You couldn't turn your back on complete strangers, people who meant nothing to you. There is no way you're walking away from this."

"You're right. Backing down from this isn't an option."

"I know. Now, we need to get our shit together, Jinn. We need a real plan," Praia spoke, still counting herself in on the mission, she had already been formally uninvited to. "Mike may be able to get us to the right place, but I have a strong feeling that it isn't going to be as simple as knocking on the door and asking for Nitara. Whoever has her is powerful enough to contain her. A djinn just like you. Sybella said you heard a witch chanting a spell. We need to figure out what spell it was."

"I believe I already know the spell. I wasn't sure at first, figured it was my mind playing games with me, but it's a familiar one." The sun was coming up soon, the last of night slipping away as the horizon turned a bright orange announcing the next morning. "I hoped like hell to never hear the damn thing again."

"What was it? Where do you know it from? That can help us piece this together, at least give us some indication of origin."

"It was used on us after we were made into djinns. That spell is what was used to bind us. It was how we became bound to our vessels." Turning his back on the sun, he looked at Praia, whose eyes were wide with excitement, calculating their next move. "They are trying to bind her."

"That wouldn't be necessary, unless..." Praia lifted her eyes. For the first time since they'd known each other Praia didn't feel like she was alone in her optimism.

"She is free," Jinn finished Praia's thought, and as unimaginable as he thought it was since he opened the envelope containing her photo, he felt a sense of relief. Nitara was free, no longer bound to her vessel. If he could get to her in time, he could make sure she remained that way.

"If she is free, that means she doesn't have to do what they wish. They're trying to bind her again so they can use her powers. Can that be done? Once you're wished free, can that be taken away?"

"I don't know. Hell, we didn't even know that we could be wished free, until I was. There is no precedent for any of this." He paused, taking his mind back to the vision Sybella gave him. "There were others there, other djinn in cages just like hers. A couple I recognized, friends from my past. Do you think it's possible? Could it be possible that they are all free?"

"That would make sense. Trap them and keep them contained until you can be sure they must obey you." Praia was now pacing the floor as her mind calculated the information she'd received. "If they are still working the spells, that means they aren't bound yet. So why haven't Nitara and the others used their powers to break free? What's stopping them?"

"The cages are enchanted. There is some powerful magic at work in there, I could feel it through the vision."

"Enchanted cages, powerful magic attempting to bind freed djinns and force them to do its bidding... yeah, this isn't going to be some cakewalk. Do you think we should call in reinforcements? There are others who would help us."

"No, it's already going to be difficult enough with the three of us going. Briar is going to prove difficult to hide." He shook his head. "I can smell her from here and the scent is only going to get stronger as the sun continues to rise."

"I should be going with you," Praia insisted, this time without the pouting face.

"Maybe, but I think we have this covered. Mike has some people on the inside who will help us out once we get there."

"You all get to go and save the day while I get the awesome duty of staying behind and babysitting. This is ridiculous!"

"Praia, I'm sure this is only the beginning of the shit we are going to have to face. Trust me, you will get your chance to kick some ass and save the day."

"Just make sure you get back here safely. Do try and keep Briar from killing Mike. The last thing we need on our hands is a murderous fairy." She headed for the door, stopped, and frowned at the bed. "Oh, and you may want to take a shower and change those sheets before you leave."

CHAPTER
TEN

"**B**oonie, baby! It's so good to see you!" The chubby man who was wrapped head to toe in tattered fabric meant to hide the appearance of his skin, wobbled up to their group. His full beard helped to further hide his discolored flesh; the sunglasses not only blocked out the sun but prevented anyone from seeing his yellowed eyes with elongated pupils. He, like so many others, didn't have the freedom of Mike, who stood with a light jacket, and V-neck shirt. The trio had arrived just moments before, having transported from Jinn's living room where a pouting Praia rolled her eyes at them, to the edges of the Collective. They were on the coast of what was once Tanzania. The smell of the Indian Ocean washed over them.

"Cole, man!" Mike greeted him with an animated bear hug that lifted the man from the ground. "Thanks for securing a landing zone for us."

"No problem, Boonie. Anything for you, my man!"

"Boonie? Why does he keep calling you that?" Briar gave Mike a side eye full of suspicion. She already lacked trust for the slither and now he was being called by a different name.

"It's my last name."

"Boonie is your last name?" She questioned again, her suspicion of him unfaltering.

"No, my last name is Boonsfield, Boonie is Cole's thing. Is that okay with you, that a friend has given me a nickname?" Mike was losing his patience with the uppity fairy.

"Cole, nice to meet you," Jinn interrupted before the two of them could take a simple conversation and turn it into more bickering.

"Jinn, I've heard a lot about you, man. You saved my man's life." Cole shook Jinn's hand and smiled. "I owe you many thanks for that."

"Yes, it seems I did, but no thanks is necessary."

"I don't mean to be rude, but we need to make this quick. We don't have much time to get you in and out of here before the shit hits the fan," Cole addressed Jinn, instinct telling him that Briar wasn't as friendly. He kept his distance and ignored her, as she did him.

"What's our route?" Mike put his arm around his friend's shoulder. "Lead the way, captain! We are all eager to get our asses out of here as quickly as possible. This isn't exactly a hotspot for vacationing."

"Underground, of course. These witches are pretty smart, but most of their protection spells are above ground. Only a few have the lower levels spelled, and if you ask me, if anyone is spelling the soil beneath their layer, that is a place you definitely don't want to be!" Cole wobbled forward about ten feet before reaching down to open a camouflaged hatch. The Earth around them was plentiful in its foliage, even in the Ashen—the witches cared for the earth, they protected it as a natural source for not only their magic, but for its ability to grow. Plants were used for potions, and animals for sacrifice. There were many rituals which depended on the Earth around them. It was in their best interest to insure its survival.

"What is this place?" Briar spoke to Cole for the first time since their arrival.

"This is safe passage, my dear." The chubby man waved at the tunnel, presenting it to them. "It's the best way to get around without being caught by those up above."

"It smells like ass," she mumbled as the air picked up, carrying the stench from the opening out into the field.

"Well, the odor of an ass, or get caught by the coven, your choice," he offered, and smiled as Mike laughed.

"How far do we have to go?"

She caved, as he knew she would. No odor was worth risking your life to avoid, no matter how rancid.

"It's going to take about a day on foot. I got us as close as I could to her without tripping any magical radars." All of the witches had them, alarms that went off if anyone using magic from outside of their coven came to visit. Jinn's magic would have set off every alarm within the Ashen had he transported them any closer.

"Is it that intense?" Mike asked. "They need alarms? I thought they had a treaty in place, no fighting. Why do they need alarm systems?"

"Man let me tell you, it has been crazy around these parts since they got the hold of this place. But they were damn brilliant in staking their claim here. Regardless of what treaties they have in place, not one of these witches are going to risk losing their homes. As I told you before, things are about to change, Boonie. We aren't the only ones preparing for it."

"Why do you say that? Why was this such a great place for them to claim?" Jinn looked around. Sure the place was beautiful, but any place could look that way with enough magic.

"The lands here are much richer with life than any other. This was the motherland, all life started here. That includes all magic. The more they nurture it, the stronger it grows. Here, even a person who has no magic can do great things if shown how. We all thought they wanted this place because at the time, no one else did. There was gold here, yes, but that wasn't going to be worth anything after the war, we all knew that. What we didn't know, is that there is so much more here, so many natural resources, ones that we had no idea about, but they did. Trust me. This place is like Fort Knox, above ground. Lately, though, more of those annoying barriers have been popping up down below as well. It's like they are on to us." He winked at Briar as she entered the hatch following Mike. Once Jinn was through, he scanned the area, making sure they weren't being watched, and disappeared beneath the soil.

"How long have you been here?" Jinn questioned Cole, who removed his wraps and shades and stuffed them into a backpack. They stood inside the hollow ground; tunnels dug by hand as the Collective had few underground passages that had existed before the war. Over the years, Cole and his people worked to expand the labyrinth as far as they could without pissing anyone off. It was hard and endless work; crews worked daily on expansion and repairs to their pathways.

"Long enough, just before they really settled in. Bounced over here from Australia about five years prior. If you ask me, this is the safest place to be. They know we are here, and as long as we keep to our areas, don't muck up their plans, we're all good. Unlike those over in the Scourge, we have better access to food, though it is still limited. This little excursion may mess that up though." He paused. "You know, if you could get this done without implementing us, that would really help us out."

"I appreciate you taking the risk. I'll try my best to keep a low profile," Jinn agreed. He didn't intend to make life harder for any of the people who lived there.

"To help my man, Boonie? Anything!" Cole chuckled as they moved ahead.

"What did you do for him to make him so loyal?" Briar asked.

"Believe it or not, I have actual friends, friends I don't have to bribe for loyalty."

"I didn't mean—" she whispered, but he stopped her.

"Yeah, okay. I know what you and your people think of me and mine. Let's just keep that shit at bay for now while we have to work together, please. I don't feel like defending myself to you throughout this entire ordeal." Mike walked ahead, matching his pace with his friend. The two quickly fell into a humorous conversation as they laughed and joked about times before the war.

"I didn't mean to offend him," she said to Jinn, who remained on pace with her.

"Didn't you though?" Jinn asked.

The first leg of their journey brought the group to a makeshift camping ground. Beneath the surface, they did the best they could to make it work. Items, mostly stolen, were brought down to create cots inside of dug-out caverns with thin, tattered sheets covering the entrances to allow for some semblance of privacy. This was their reality; this was the life Mike wanted to get his child away from.

"I never really thought about how they lived down here all these years." Briar watched a family of four shuffle past their group and head down a tunnel that lead east of them, where Cole said the majority of their people stayed.

Cole announced that he had chosen housing away from the general population when he learned that Briar was coming. It was a better bet to keep them separate and avoid any misunderstandings. A fairy appearing in their world wasn't going to be taken as a good thing.

"We tend not to think about the things that make us uncomfortable," Jinn offered as he laid down a blanket over the pallet. "Don't beat yourself up about it."

"Mike, he grew up like this?" She adjusted her own bedding as they spoke.

"Born and raised. His parents were some of the first to have to take to the sewers. Unless you're in an area where snakes, alligators, and crocodiles are common, you have to hide. Even then, it's not as if they are out and about with everyone else."

"I never really knew what they were, their deformity." Though they were given the name slithers, not all of them shifted to snakes. A few, like Mike, could take on the form of multiple reptiles though he had his preference for the anaconda.

"They are shifters, gone wrong. The failed experiment of a young witch trying to make something unnatural happen." Jinn looked at Mike pensively before he continued to relay the history that wasn't his own. "Mike's parents were at a resort, vacationing. They'd just gotten married. As far as I understand it, the witch came out of nowhere with her spell. She wasn't provoked, just bored, is more likely. Nearly everyone at the resort, some five hundred people were changed that day. They didn't know it, though. They left, went back to their normal lives, business as usual. It took a few weeks for the effects to really show. It wasn't long after that when they realized they would have to hide. Mike's mother got the worst of it. Her body deformed—half human, half reptile—but his father loved her, and stayed by her side."

"Mike was born this way?"

"Yes, and to be honest, he's a lot better off than anyone would have expected. Unlike those before him, his generation can actually shift from a bi-pedaled form to others, but as you can see, his skin is still not quite what you would expect of a human." They were alone, Mike had gone off with Cole to allow the two of them time to settle in, and to give himself a breather from the judgement of Briar.

"Damn. Well, I feel like shit now."

"Why?"

"I've judged him, and those like him, all of this time. I never knew." Her eyes followed the path of the hall that led east. "That family, their children, they've probably never seen the light of day, or played in a field. It's so beautiful up there and they are stuck down here, fearing for their lives."

"Well, we often make unfortunate judgements, based on biased information. That is, until we take the time to educate ourselves.

Maybe you can use this experience to do that, learn more about these people and their lives. Outside of what you were told before." Without realizing it, Jinn had already started to help Mike. Briar was listening to him, considering his words.

"We got grub!" Mike announced as he returned with armfuls of nearly expired food and some that were far past their prime.

"We're going to eat this?" Briar picked up a piece of overly ripe fruit from the pile of food that Cole laid out before her.

"Let me guess, not good enough for your highness?" Mike huffed.

"I j-just m-meant," she stammered, trying to find the appropriate words. "This isn't right, I mean…"

"No worries," Jinn stepped in, saving Briar from her bumbling mind. He waved his hand over the haul. Before their eyes spoiled products turned to new—including the piece of fruit in Briar's hand. "Sorry, but I have to agree with Briar, tempting sour stomachs the night before going into battle isn't a great idea."

"Whoa." Cole picked up a handful of food. "You think you can do that for some of the others down here? I hate to ask this of you, but I mean, these people haven't had a decent meal in, well, ever."

"After all of your help, I would be happy to." He paused. "What about risking setting off the magical alarms? This wasn't much, but a large-scale change will put out a lot of energy."

"Oh, we are still outside of the barriers, it should be fine." Cole wasn't entirely sure of their proximity to alarms, but he couldn't pass up the chance of getting his people fresh food.

"Well, by all means, lead the way."

"Thanks. You have no idea how much this is going to mean to them, especially the kids." Cole chattered on as he headed off down the tunnel that led to the general population. Jinn followed behind him.

The tunnel was about fifty feet long, and at the end of it was a large cavern that went deeper into the ground. A stairwell carved into the walls was the path down from the entrance to the bottom of the cavern where everyone sat. As they entered, slithers of all sorts watched them. Cole grinned. He would be celebrated forever as the one who brought the djinn who fed them like kings for a night.

"Everyone! Please gather around!" He gained the attention of the group quickly.

"Cole, who is this?" A lanky man asked with a voice that possessed more bass than his gangly form would suggest.

"Jeremy, before you freak out, I know that none of us like unexpected visitors, but trust me, he is okay."

"That doesn't tell us who he is," Jeremey insisted as he looked Jinn up and down.

"My name is Jinn." The visitor spoke up for himself; there was nothing worse than being talked about like you weren't in the room.

"Jinn, as in Jinn the djinn?" Jeremey asked. "Funny about that naming, huh?"

"I can't say I hear the differences in the words, but yeah, that's me." He'd learned laugh at the coincidence of his name and what he was turned into a long time ago. If he'd let it bother him every time someone pointed it out, he'd spend a lot of time pissed off. For someone who was set to live and eternity, that wasn't a good outlook. "Look, Cole here has offered to help me and my friends out, and I would like to return the favor."

"How?" A small voice questioned, a little girl who held a piece of what looked like week-old bread from the green spots on it.

"Like this." Jinn walked over to the girl, knelt down in front of her, and turned the bread into a fresh roll. It warmed in her hand, feeling as if fresh from the oven. The smell rose from the cooked dough, filling the room. "Try it." He smiled at her and she lifted the loaf to her nose.

"It smells so good." Her eyes grew wide, she had never known that smell. "I've never smelled anything so good before."

"It tastes even better." He nodded. "Go ahead, take a bite."

As the small girl bit into the bread, everyone in the space inhaled, waiting for her verdict. At first it seemed she might be unfavorable to the taste she had never experienced before. But the skeptical frown that marked her face gradually turned into a smile. "It's so good! Can you make more?" She beamed and Jinn nodded.

"I'll make as much as you like."

CHAPTER
ELEVEN

"I'm sorry," Briar told Mike as she picked up a piece of fruit. The cheers echoed through the tunnels; Jinn must have been working his magic.

"What do you have to apologize about?" Mike sat down after getting his cot as comfortable as it was going to get.

"Being a bitch to you all this time. I don't mean to be."

"It's fine." He picked up a fresh piece of bread, popped it into his mouth, and groaned, then chose another piece of fruit.

"No, it isn't. You didn't choose the cards you were dealt. It's not my place to hold any of this against you. It's just hard to separate the things I've heard, from what is the apparent truth." She waited before continuing. Mike lifted his eyes to her; he was listening. "I grew up being told about how horrible you and others like you were. Those stories told of thieves who were aggressive and abusive, monsters who preyed on my kind. I see now that what I was told, what I was taught, isn't the truth, at least not about all of you. I will try harder to judge you solely on the person you are, and not the stories I've been told all of these years."

"You know, you could try not to judge me at all." He winked at her before handing her half of the loaf of bread he'd been chomping on, an offer of peace.

She accepted it and pulled a piece from the loaf, popping it into her mouth. "Yes, I could, but we both know that I would fail." She grinned.

"True. I guess I will have to take what I can get." Standing up, he stretched his arms over his head. "Look, you aren't the only one with preconceived notions. You're not exactly what I thought a fairy to be."

"I'm not?"

"No, you're much worse." He laughed so hard at his own joke he snorted.

"Very funny. Where are you from, Mike?" Briar pulled a bottle of water from her backpack, drank half of its contents, and offered the other half to Mike who eagerly accepted the chance for hydration.

"Well, I was born in New York, but I'm not really from anywhere. My family, my people, we don't ever really lay down roots, it's a life of a nomad. Stay in one place too long and you get caught up. It's different now, at least we get to call someplace home, not that home is something worth bragging about. It's just good to be able to go back to the same place every night, see the same people."

"Do you have a family?"

"Yes. My parents died a while back, they didn't make it through the war, but I have three brothers and a sister." He paused, as if considering how much he wanted to tell the woman who had yet to earn his trust. Briar wondered how much he would share with her. She understood why he wouldn't want to, but apparently, he decided it was worth continuing. "My wife and I are expecting a little girl now."

"Really?" Briar smiled.

"Yeah, in just a few weeks someone will be calling me daddy." He chuckled. "You know, a few years ago the thought of being called daddy had an entirely different effect on me. I'm looking forward to it, though. My wife, Iris, that woman is absolutely amazing. I can't imagine my life without her. Now, my focus is just trying to provide something better for her, and for our daughter."

"That's intense."

"Tell me about it. Why do you think I'm here?" He looked around the tunnel and thought of the angry witches above ground who would like nothing more than to dissect them all. "I mean, I care about Jinn and his wife, really, but risking my life to save a chick I don't even know just weeks before my child is born, that isn't exactly a smart idea. I have bigger plans, a hope for change, and I'm hoping like hell that Jinn can help me do that."

"That is noble of you." She wondered if she would be able to do the same, put so much on the line, as he was.

"Noble, yeah. I guess that's one way of looking at it." He sighed. "Some might call it selfish."

"Looks like you two are getting along." Cole walked in, chest puffed out, and head held high.

"Where is Jinn?" Briar glanced behind him and saw no one. She stood, ready to fight if needed.

"Oh, he is coming, just saying his final good-byes." Cole smiled to ease the tense warrior.

"You look mighty proud of yourself, old friend." Mike patted the chubby man on the back.

"They will revere me." He laughed. "They will speak my name and think of the great gift I brought upon them."

"Is that so?" Mike peered around him. "I don't see anyone revering you."

Cheers from the festive slithers echoed down the tunnel. "You hear that? All of them, so happy, bellies full, and they will think of one name when they think of this night."

"Jinn! Jinn! Jinn!" The crowd cheered on.

"Doesn't sound to me like they are shouting your name, buddy."

"Well, those ungrateful…" Cole huffed.

"Ah, don't let it bother you. We all know who the real hero of the night is, and it isn't the man with hands of magic that turn rotted food into a feast meant for a king. It's you!"

"You know, he conjured up steaks, magically, perfectly cooked steaks." Cole was drooling. "I haven't had one of those in a very long time."

"Steaks? Um… I'll be right back!" Mike took off running toward the sound of cheers, hoping to get a fresh T-bone for himself.

"Some friend he is. They ate them all anyway," he muttered, and Briar laughed.

"That guy has some real issues." Jinn laughed as he appeared in the corner behind Briar. "Sorry, I had to get out of there. You know Mike came running in and dived at the table of steaks? It's a good thing I conjured more, or he would have likely killed that little girl for her piece."

"Yeah, more steaks, great," Cole mumbled. "I need to go check the guard posts. I'll be back." He sauntered off.

"What's wrong with him?"

"I think he really wanted to be the hero of the night, and well, the steaks kinda overshadowed him."

"Oh, steaks have a way of doing that. Why do you think I left Praia with so many of them?" He laughed. The steaks had been his way of apologizing for putting her on babysitting duty. If he ever needed her to forget about something, he just had to plop down a fat prime cut in front of her.

"I spoke with Mike."

"Yeah? How ugly did it get?"

"Surprisingly, it went well." She paused, as if recalling their conversation. "You're right. I need to educate myself more on him and his people. A lot of my people need to do the same."

"Well, it's a start."

"Man, you sure do know how to conjure up a mean steak!" Mike walked back into their little dugout with two steaks in hand while he chewed on the rest of another.

Jinn laughed. "You are a heathen, Mike."

"What? You know as well as I do, steak is a rare commodity. Sure, it may not be the real thing, but it tastes just as good!"

"Not the real thing?" Briar asked.

"Well, it's magic. It isn't carved from an actual cow," Jinn offered.

"You mean to tell me you happily eat fake food?" She looked at Mike, who started on the next slab of meat.

"Hell, tastes good, and fills my belly. What's fake about that?" He grinned around the mouthful.

"Huh, so this bread, not real?" She lifted the bread from the platter.

"The bread is real. It's a time isolation spell." Jinn picked up a piece for himself. "I reversed time, for just the target intended, in this case, a loaf of rye."

"After eating rotted fruit for years and having to pick around the parts the flies beat you to, a piece of fake steak. Bread reversed in time is the best a man can get down here!" The slither sat down on his cot and finished off his meal. He offered Briar a piece of the meat, but she declined.

Jinn took this as his time to exit. He left the two to have what would be the most normal conversation he'd heard the two of them have since meeting. His designated nook waited for him with a cot that sat in the far corner. Walls of compacted dirt muffled most of their conversation and gave him enough quiet so that he could meditate. Providing a night of happiness, of good food and peace of mind for others was great, but he had so much more to worry about. In less than a day he would be face-to-face with her, and with his fear that she no longer loved him. As much as Mike's bickering with Briar, the temporary underground lifestyle, and the shit he would most likely be stirring up with the fairies by helping the slithers all weighed on his mind, nothing was heavier than that of his concern for Nitara. He cleared his head, centered himself in his magic, and escaped the world, back to her, when she loved him without condition, without fault. Her smile was his breath, her eyes, his heartbeat. Her every imperfection, his reason for living. He loved her without regard for himself. It was those moments he needed to hold on to, those moments would be the ones to push him forward when shit got real, to save her life, even if she made it clear that she wanted nothing to do with him.

CHAPTER
TWELVE

"I hope you all are rested up and ready to go! We have a lot of ground to cover," Cole announced as he approached the three of them. They were up and ready to start the next leg of their journey.

"What happened to you last night, I thought you were coming back?" Mike stood, worried about his friend. Cole always kept his word; his absence had thrown the man off.

"I intended to, but it seems one of the checkpoints was overtaken, which means we have been rerouted." Cole omitted how it was overtaken and no one asked. They assumed he meant the witches.

"Rerouted?" The fairy asked, confirming what she overheard.

"Yes, unfortunately." Briar rolled her eyes and Mike huffed. "Rest assured, we still have safe passage. This is just a minor setback."

Jinn exited his makeshift room. "How minor?"

"A few hours, tops," Cole quickly responded.

"Great, then I suggest we get going." Jinn picked up the bag that held the few possessions he brought.

"Yes, but first we need to go over a few things." Cole sat down on the ground, inviting the others to join him. "I thought this might be helpful for all of you. This is the place we're headed." Cole rolled out the large blueprint.

"How did you get this?" Mike peered over the plans of a massive home.

"Witches didn't seem too concerned with public records when they took over. There is a building that stores blueprints for every structure within a hundred-mile radius."

"So what are we looking at?" Jinn swept his eyes over the blueprint laid out on the ground.

"The home is large, but lucky for us, access to the basement is pretty easy. Head through the front door and make it down the hall straight ahead. Access to the basement is the second door on your left."

"Have you been inside before?" Mike doubted his friend was that brave or that foolish.

"Me, no, but some of the humans up there, the ones they haven't chopped up, they help us. That is how I got the picture."

"Thank you for this." Jinn stood. "It will make this easier

knowing exactly how to get to her."

Mike and Briar gathered their things, they made sure that nothing was left behind and strapped their packs on tight. As the group headed off with Cole at the lead, they passed a family who smiled at Jinn, thanking him for his gifts of the previous night. Briar smiled at them as she passed, but all but the children shied away. The little girl, who looked wide eyed and happy with her belly full for the first time since she was born, smiled at Briar and eyed the bottle of water she held in her hand. Briar handed the water to the girl who happily accepted it. Though her mother relaxed, happy that her daughter would have proper hydration, her father still bristled. Well, it was a start.

"You think they will ever trust us?" Briar whispered to Jinn as they walked past more slithers, all of whom shied away from the fairy. "I mean, these people, there isn't much I can do, but I hope that one day, they have a better way of living."

"You hoping for change is a start. Maybe that hope can spread from you to the others in Vilar. Perhaps Mike's dream of a better way for his people doesn't have to be that far-fetched at all."

"I wish there was more that I could do." Though she was high in command of the guard, she made no real impact on the queen's choices. At the end of the day, Briar was just another person in line to protect Alesea.

"There is, you can start the conversation, or at least help it start."

"So, he was telling the truth last night. He said all he wanted was a way to make a change for his people. He wants to start a conversation, a bargain." She kept her eyes trained on Mike's back, but Jinn knew that it was because it was easier than watching person after person pull away from her like she was coming to steal their young. Bringing her to the tunnels had been a good idea, not just to help save Nitara, but it was opening her mind. "I'm not sure that I can help much with that."

"That is what he told me." Jinn nodded. "My role in all of this is to get him in front of Alesea."

"If anyone can do that, it's you." She adjusted the pack on her back. "Hell, I've never seen anyone waltz into Vilar, head straight for the crown, demand time with the queen, and walk out as if it was nothing out of the ordinary. Not only that, but she granted you remote access to the Seer and the dedicated assistance of her second in command." She paused and looked up at him. "Now, tell me, how exactly did you manage to pull that off?"

"Um, guys, we may have a bit of a problem here!" Mike called out, eliminating any response Jinn might have given the fairy—not that it would have been all that revealing.

"What is it, Mike?" Jinn shrugged and left Briar grateful for the rescue from their conversation.

"It seems our easy pathway no longer exists." He nodded to the wall of dirt blocking their way, the tunnel having freshly collapsed.

"I thought you said this way was better?" Jinn turned to Cole, holding his temper back, but his aggravation was clear as the clear blue sky they couldn't see above them.

"Th-this wasn't h-here y-yesterday," Cole stammered. "I s-swear! That is why it took me so long to get back, I spent the entire night mapping out a new route!"

"So what do you suggest we do about this?" Mike walked up, laying his hand on the fresh wall. Before Cole could warn him about his actions, a spark of power blasted Mike and sent him flying five feet back across the space where he landed in the sure arms of Briar. The woman made a solid catch without so much as a back step.

"Well, aren't you the mighty one." He gazed up at her with a dazzling smile.

"Sun's up, so is my strength." Briar shrugged as Mike regained proper footing.

"What the hell was that?" He looked at Cole, who wore a grimace.

"It's magic, a protection spell. Cross it and we're fried."

"Yeah, see, that is what we call pertinent information." Mike scoured at his friend. "It would have been useful about thirty seconds ago, buddy."

"Sorry." Cole cut his eyes to the ground and held back his laughter. Mike's hair was standing from his head as residual static from the shock ran through him.

"Shit, what are we going to do?" Briar kept an eye on Jinn, whose jaw had become so rigid they might have been able to use it to cut through the barrier.

"We're going to go around it and hope like hell the secondary pass isn't blocked as well. If it is… well, to put it simply, we're screwed. This is going to cost us some more time though." It was obvious by his expression that Cole was afraid to say the words, knowing the message would not be well received.

"How much more time?" Jinn growled through his tightened jaw.

Cole hesitated to answer him, but when Jinn's angered eyes reached him, he coughed up the information. "At least a few hours."

"We need to move faster than that, we don't have any more time to waste playing maze runner down here. We need Briar at her best when this happens," Jinn stated. The longer it took to get to Nitara, the worse off they were. Though Briar would still be useful after sunset, her strength would diminish greatly.

"Get us close enough," Briar spoke to Cole before directing his gaze at the djinn who was turning an unsettling shade of red. "After we are close enough, then, Jinn, you can work some magic and make up the difference."

"Isn't that going to trigger some magical alarm?" Mike offered.

"Frankly, I don't give a damn," Jinn barked as Cole headed down another passage. "Let's move!" He called out as he forged ahead. Mike and Briar followed him closely

"You think we should be worried about him?" Briar whispered, having kept a good distance between herself and the cherry-colored djinn.

"Jinn? No, I'm sure he is all right." Mike shrugged, but just two days prior his back had been slammed against a workbench in Jinn's garage with the angry man ahead of them holding him in place. "The man's just a bit on edge. This is his wife, after all, the love of his life. It's bound to get under his skin, don't you think?"

"Yeah, sure, I suppose. Still, I think we need to be careful, make sure he doesn't go falling off that edge he seems to be balancing on."

꒰ J ꒱

"Okay, so it's been about three minutes since Jinn jumped us here, and no reign of terror yet. Good news, right?" It was obvious Mike was still trying to catch his breath from the surge of power that shot them through the maze of underground tunnels. He only puked once, so he wouldn't have to turn in his man card just yet.

"I can't say." Cole hadn't handled the ride with as much grace as Mike. He left every bit of food he'd eaten under a neat pile of dirt and was still green in the face… more so than usual. "We need to stay on our toes, just in case. Just because nothing blew up, doesn't mean they aren't setting traps."

"Good way of looking at this. Stay alert," Briar announced, and frowned at Mike. "Um, you have a little something on your chin." She pointed at the remnants of puke he'd missed when cleaning his face.

"Oh, thanks." He wiped his face. "Jinn, you okay? You've been quiet."

"Yeah, I'm fine, just trying to stay focused here." He pulled his hair back, replacing the few strands which had come free during transport. "Cole, how much further do we have to go now?"

"We're actually pretty close, maybe fifteen minutes walking."

"Good, lead the way."

"Shit!" Cole grumbled as he felt the familiar vibrations beneath his feet.

"Cole, what's the problem?" Briar ran to his side, if he was still sick from Jinn's magic, she could use some of her own to counteract the effect.

"We gotta get out of here," he whispered.

"What?" Mike called over.

"They're coming!" Cole panicked, looking for an exit strategy. "We need to get away from here, and quickly."

"Who?" Mike grabbed him by the collar, forcing him to look him in the eye. "What the hell is going on, Cole? Who is coming?"

"The fucking gloamers! They're the result of some fucked up experiments that happened in the Ashen. Those things were unleashed down here about two months ago. It wasn't bad before… just a few of them. We learned to keep our distance, avoid them at all cost, but the damn things multiply like fucking rats. Every time we look up, there are more of them."

"What are they?" Mike questioned further. "Are they like us? What do they want?"

"Mike, I have no idea. It's like someone was up there playing mad scientist, crossing different animals, different species, both supernatural and not. They aren't anything like us, but there is something else."

"What?" Mike's voice carried the worry that they all felt. If Cole was calling him anything but Boonie, it meant they were really in for some shit.

"Pretty sure they used some bits and pieces borrowed from their human pets." He swallowed. "Like some crazy ass chop shop."

"What?" Jinn pushed between them. "What do you mean bits of human?"

"Their faces, man. They are all mutilated, but clearly, they are human in some parts, like masks stretched over the faces of monster. Some of them have the hands and feet of humans, others have paws or hooves. The shit is sick. They're out to kill, man, they're out for blood. They rip through anyone they come in contact with."

"Fuck." Mike turned to Jinn. "You think they would have learned the lesson after what happened to all of us." He punched the wall.

"Yeah, we need to move," Cole repeated.

"How do you know those things are coming? How can you tell?" Briar asked Cole, trying to bring him back to focus. The man looked like he would pass out, and that was the last thing they needed.

"I can feel them in the ground."

"He's right, they aren't too far from us now," Mike co-signed. "Looks like we did set off some magical alarms after all."

"Well, since we've been found out, I guess it doesn't matter what we do next." Jinn smiled, grabbing Mike's shoulder and Briar's hand. "Make sure you hold on to him," he instructed her, nodding at Cole. "And watch out for the upchuck."

CHAPTER
THIRTEEN

"You think they would learn about trying to play god," Briar mumbled as she did her best to clean the green slime from her shoe. Cole really had an issue keeping his lunch down. She didn't understand how the man had anything left to throw up.

"We're in the dark zone, sweetheart. They don't think they're playing god… here they think they are god." Mike offered her a dingy rag to help with the clean-up.

"What they are doing here is sick! How can the others just stand by and let it happen? Why has no one intervened?" More of the horrors of the world were being revealed to her than she thought she could handle. Even as the head of the queen's guard, she was still sheltered from what existed outside of the limits of Vilar.

"Yeah, don't I know it." Mike waved his hands around at their current location. They were literally crawling through tunnels where people lived. Talk about an injustice! "You gotta realize, they have peace here. If that means a few humans get sliced up for weird experiments, that is just a part of the bargain. It keeps that treaty intact. If someone was to try to go against that, it means another war. I don't know about you, but I damn sure don't want to go through another one of those."

"Yeah, you're right." No one wanted war again. "Something needs to be done, though. This can't be allowed."

"Well, if we make it out of here alive, maybe you can petition the queen to step in," Mike suggested, reinforcing his agenda.

"We're here," a pale, sweaty faced Cole announced, pointing above him. "This hatch here, you will come up just a few yards away from the home. It's hard to miss, large and gothic. I will wait for you here."

"Thank you, Cole." Jinn shook his hand.

"No problem." Cole nervously wiped the sweat from his brow. "No problem at all. I'll wait here for you to return." As much as he wanted to help, he couldn't take the chance of being seen with them. After they were done, they would pop back to safety, and he would have to live with the consequences.

Above ground now, they kept low to the ground as they moved between trees, making sure no one saw them approaching.

"Something isn't right here," Briar said as they moved closer to the home.

"What do you mean?" Mike stopped; wide eyes found her face. "You think they have land mines or some shit out here?"

"There is no one here. No guards, henchmen, nothing. I can't sense one person within close proximity of this location." She inhaled the air, allowing her smell and ears to take over for sight. There was nothing, as if the area had been abandoned.

"You think we're in the wrong place?" Jinn looked around, noting the inconsistencies. Briar was right—not one person was on duty, giving them a clear path to just walk up to the door. It could have been a setup.

"No, Cole knows this place. If he says this is where we need to be, then it's where we need to be." Mike looked around, noting the lack of activity even in the neighboring buildings. "She's right, something is definitely not right here."

Jinn left the cover of the shadows and ran for the building that was known to house his love. The Earth around the house was dead. Relics of grass and weeds crushed beneath his feet as he ran.

"Jinn, what the hell?" Mike called out in a frantic whisper before both he and Briar followed suit. If it were a setup, they were already compromised, and if not, Jinn's mad dash for the door did that for them.

They ran, scanning the area, expecting to be ambushed, but

nothing happened. No one jumped out of the corner with bullets, arrows, or any other form of assault. Without incident, they made it to the oversized door of the building built from distressed brick and pillars that held high arches along the extended porch. Jinn opted out of politely knocking and kicked in the door. He dove through the opening, ready for a fight, but inside, there was nothing. Met with the eerie absence of sound, he followed the directions given to him and headed straight for the basement where Nitara was being held. His gut told him he was too late, that there was no point in going down the stairs. If the place was empty, she wouldn't be there, or worse, he would find her, lifeless.

When Briar and Mike finally caught up to him, they found him on his knees in a dank, wet, musty basement surrounded by cages, all empty.

"She was here, right here," Jinn whispered.

"Shit." Briar hit the wall. "We're too late."

"Maybe this is the wrong place," Mike offered, knowing Jinn's mind would be taking him down the worst possible path.

"No, she was here." The man lifted himself from the ground, turning to his partners with his hand open. In his palm, the crescent moon, his gift to his wife, one she never removed. "They're gone." Jinn looked at Mike when no one responded. "Where are they?" He yelled and grabbed the messenger, the one who brought hope back into his life. He lifted him by the collar away from the ground and slammed him against the wall. "Where are they?" He screamed. "Tell me where she is!"

"Jinn, man, I don't know. I'm sorry." Mike didn't resist—he hung there, waiting for Jinn to come to his senses. If he put up any fight it might have agitated the situation even more.

"Jinn, stop, please," Briar pleaded. "Let him go, we have to get out of here. Everyone is gone, not just Nitara, which means they have relocated, and whatever the hell they are planning hasn't happened yet. If it did, something tells me we would all know about it. Whatever is being planned here, it's big, the kind of scheme that would change the world, not just the lives of a few witches."

Briar made sense and as her logic began to outweigh the roller coaster of emotions that she knew he was experiencing. Jinn relaxed and released his hold on Mike who fell back to the ground. He stepped back from his friend, dropping his gaze down to his hand where the gift he'd made for his wife still rested in his palm. *Why isn't she wearing it? What did they do to her?*

"Look, we will find her," Mike reassured. "We will, but Briar is right. We need to go. Just because whoever it is that owns this place isn't here now, it doesn't mean it isn't under surveillance or that they won't be back. We need to move. We need to get out of here."

Jinn nodded. "Yeah, okay, let's go."

"We should look around first, see if we can find anything to help us figure this out," Briar suggested, and though they searched the basement, they came up empty, only finding old rags and chalk. The place had been wiped clean.

After the search that left them no more informed, they headed for the exit. With only two hours before the sun would set, they needed to get as far away from the house as possible. Mike and Briar ran ahead, scoping the area and making sure Cole was still waiting for them.

"What's wrong?" Briar had turned back after noticing Jinn's absence. She found him standing in the foyer, a dark cloth in his hand, and an expression of pure anger on his face that worried her.

"This symbol, I know it." He held the cloth out for her to see it. On the dark fabric was a gold symbol—the letter D doubled onto itself and encircled in two gold rings.

"You do?" She studied the fabric. "Where is it from?"

"Yes, I've seen it before, up close and personal." His voice grew darker as he spoke.

"What?" She pulled her eyes from the fabric. "What do you mean up close and personal? Do you know who this belongs to?"

"I know who has Nitara, and when I get my hands on him, I'm going to kill him." He snatched the fabric from the fairy.

Briar nodded. "Well, good. We need to get out of here, Jinn."

"Yeah, I'm coming."

Briar backed out of the room, once again exiting the house.

Jinn crumpled the fabric in his hand. He thought of his wife, and of the bastard who had her. With the fire of his rage, the cloth burst into flames. He dropped it to the floor, and as he left, he held his hand out to spread more of the flames. As they disappeared into the ground, returning to the hidden tunnels, the home crumbled from within, engulfed by the flames.

FOURTEEN

"**Y**ou going to tell us what that was about?" Briar questioned Jinn as soon as they had made it a safe distance from the burning house. "Who has Nitara?"

"Someone from our past," the djinn mumbled.

"Your past… care to be a little more specific?" She tried her best to keep her tone calm. She had to approach the issue with a level head, or they would get nowhere. "Look, I know this is hard, and if this was a different situation, I wouldn't pry, but we need to know whatever it is you know. We have to figure out what we're up against with this."

"His name is Daegal, he is a warlock."

They continued moving with Cole leading the way. He took his time to steer them clear of any traps.

"Daegal… I've never heard of him," Mike offered. He kept well informed of the heavy hitters, the major players, anyone that may have proven a threat to him and his people. The name Jinn mentioned had never come up.

"He was never one for show, always kept to himself. I wouldn't be surprised if he is using a different name now. But that symbol, it's his. I would recognize it anywhere."

"Okay, so how do you know him?" Briar kept pace with Jinn. "You said he is from your past, when did you cross paths with someone so terrible?"

"He is the one who turned us, Nitara and I. He is the one who made us what we are now."

"You mean, he turned you into djinns?" Mike stopped walking and looked at his friend. "You weren't always a djinn?"

"No, we weren't. We were made this. Before Daegal attacked, we were witches, farmers. He condemned a local town. At the time we thought he was just there to terrorize the people. A lot of witches had gone rogue at the time, lashed out at the human population. Some were doing it out of fear, others out of hate, and some just for the fun of it, but it became clear his intentions were something different entirely."

"Meaning?" The group had proceeded again, following Cole down a path that became tighter as they moved forward.

"He was looking for a lot more than just being a pain in the ass for the locals. I stepped in, interfered, thought I could help those people. Had I known what I know now, I might not have stepped in at all." He swallowed the lump of guilt that formed in his throat. "It turned out that his intention was to draw out witches who would be foolish enough to try to help the humans. He preyed on the kind hearted. Anyone who would stand up against an unknown enemy and take the heat for a village whom they barely knew, was someone he wanted. Once I stepped up, defended those people, he left the town alone and came after us. We ran but didn't get far before he found us."

"Why the hell would he want to make you a djinn?" Mike blurted out. "Hell, how did he have the power to do that? I mean, you're essentially a demon, right?"

"Something like that. He used dark magic, and a lot of it." As far as everyone knew, the djinn were demons. They were tricksters who used their magic to turn wishes into punishments. Daegal wanted his own special brand of djinn; he wanted them to grant his wishes without consequence.

"Clearly he was playing a long game. Think about how many djinns he made, and all this time later, he just now wants to collect and cash in." Briar was turning over the pieces in her mind. "He had something in the works all that long ago? Do you think he wants you too?"

"How is he still alive? As far as I knew, witches weren't immortal," Mike spouted off more questions. A warlock powerful enough to make magical demons was not something he wanted to mess with. Thoughts of his unborn daughter and the wife he'd left behind came to him. He wanted to provide a better future for them, but he also wanted to be a part of their future.

"Well, if he is using dark magic, we can be sure that has something to do with the longevity of his life. There is no telling what type of shit he is in, or what bargains he has made for immortality." Briar shook her head, wiping sweat from her brow. The sun was lowering, and her temperature was rising. It had been too long underneath the ground, and the few moments in the sun were not enough. If she didn't get home soon, she would get sick.

"So, we know who our target is, that's a leg up. Maybe some of my contacts have information on this guy that we can use to our advantage." As much as he wanted to turn and run, Mike swallowed the bullet. He was already in the thick of it, better to play his part or risk proving what everyone already thought of his people. He chose a side and he had to stick with it.

"Yes, and I will use our archives. If anyone has come into contact with him, it would have been logged for our records. No way someone this evil could have flown under our radar entirely. Right now, we just have to get home. Sybella can help as well, but she will need you to be there so she can tap into your memory." Briar's mind was working a mile a minute, as was Mike's, who gave Cole a list of directives for who to reach out to once they'd gone.

"Shit!" Cole, who had remained silent in order to not get any further involved in the mess, stopped in his tracks. "Gloamers!"

This time it was too late for them to avoid the oncoming threat. Just up ahead the left side of the tunnel exploded and through the opening, with a thundering sound of growls and shrieks of hunger, poured in mutated beings.

"Run!" Mike yelled as the creatures stormed the tunnel headed for them. The four retreated, backing up into a large, hollowed-out zone, previously inhabited by more of Cole's people, but once the gloamers moved in, they evacuated the area. The evil that created them was the type to poison everything around it.

"This isn't right!" Cole shouted as he pressed his back up against the wall. "It's like they are acting on command, like they were sent here for us."

"This isn't normal?" Jinn questioned.

"No, I've never seen more than a few of them together at a time. That has to be just about every damn one of those things that are down here!"

"Well, I guess we know who created them!" Jinn placed his hand on the entrance to the tunnel. The mutated creatures were closing in on them. "Get back!" He yelled, and then slammed his fist into the carved entrance. The opening collapsed, sealing their predators outside, but this left them trapped. On the other side, they could hear frantic digging—the gloamers were trying to get through. "Well, that buys us a little time."

"This isn't right, they are different now," Cole continued his panicked assessment of the monsters' behavior.

"What do you mean?" Briar prepared herself, centering the remaining power she'd drawn from the sun.

"Usually they would just turn away, give up, and go find another meal option. They aren't stopping."

"Meal option?" Mike spat. "What the hell do you mean?"

"Yeah, they aren't just murderers, they are hunting for food. The damn things never stop. Usually they find animals, some that we hunt and leave for them."

"You feed them?" Mike turned on his friend, disgust with his revelation evident on his face.

"It's either feed them or get eaten."

"Oh hell no! I am not going to be a part of some freak's dinner plan!" Briar screamed at the wall that stood as a barrier between them and the things that planned to have them as a meal.

"What are we going to do?" Cole muttered as he searched hopelessly for a way out. His fear stunk as much as the sweat that poured from his chubby brow.

"We're going to fight. Get ready, they are almost through." Mike stepped forward, then turned to Cole. "Get back, stay low." Cole was great at many things, but fighting wasn't one of them. If he stayed out of the way it would mean less of a distraction.

"Mike," Briar stepped forward, "you know how to kill these things?"

"No, but in my experience, removing the head has always been a surefire way. Hope you got enough charge from the sun while we were up there."

Briar held up her hands, and two long blades of light appeared. "I got plenty."

Jinn remained where he was, focusing on the sound of the monsters trying to get through. As he stared ahead, he steadied his breathing, blocking out all sound, all senses focused on the goal: kill as many of those bastards as he could. They were almost through—the temporary blockage began to crumble, lifting more dust into the air. He took one deep breath as the last of the barrier fell away.

The gloamers poured through, making their way quickly Briar and Mike, who lunged forward and engaged in physical combat. Mike shifted his form; instead of taking on that of his favorite, the anaconda, he became a large, mutated crocodile. The only thing different between him and a regular crocodile was the length of his legs. His were about twice the size, and that gave him the agility he needed to quickly move between the monsters. His powerful jaw snapped repeatedly, breaking bones, and ripping flesh. The creatures screamed in pain as his teeth cut through them, while his tail whipped around with precision, knocking them down.

Briar kept in tow, doing exactly what Mike suggested and removing their heads. Her blades sliced through necks, torsos, limbs, anything they came in contact with, sending the orange blood splattering around her. Each shriek of pain fueled her to continue, each mutant death was a step closer to her own survival. She kept an eye on Mike, afraid one would catch him off guard, but every time she checked for him, she found large teeth cutting through tendons, ripping heads from bodies, and leaving disfigured forms littered in his wake.

Cole ducked further into the back of the space, finding a small nook to crawl into. The gloamers were starting to get past Mike and Briar, and yet not one had approached Jinn, as if he wasn't in the room. They flooded the area, parting as they ran around Jinn, unquestioning the action. Jinn watched as the pair worked together as they continued to cut down their enemy. He intentionally held off his attack. He hoped that allowing them to fight, side by side, would inspire a growth in their relationship. If their kind was ever to come to an agreement, knowing that they could trust one another on the battlefield was key. It wasn't until the creatures made it deeper into the space, nearly surrounding the two fighters, that he decided to step in. Two steps and a leap planted him in the center of the fight. The anger that burned through him, the rage he had been suppressing for nearly a week was released in a storm of heated action. He snapped necks with one hand, broke limbs, and ripped hearts from their chest. More and more came and still he fought, enjoying the physical nature of the act. Magic was easy, but taking them on, hand to hand, it gave him joy, pleasure.

"Jinn!" Briar was down, on her back, her swords the only thing protecting her neck from the teeth of the thing on top of her. Mike was also cornered, hideous creatures coming at him from all sides. Jinn followed her line of sight and realized quickly that his time of enjoyment had to come to an end, or one of their lives would.

"Stay down!" He yelled, giving his friends only a moment of notice before lifting his hand up and releasing a stream of blue flames which ripped out into the space. The blade of fire sliced through and burned everything it touched. He controlled the flame, making sure not to hurt those who were on his side. He lifted his other hand, aiming for the point of the gloamers' entry, and shot an identical stream of fire through the opening. Anything that was trying to get in was burned, flesh melted away as they continued to try to enter regardless of their unavoidable deaths. The blaze sustained until there were no more cries of agony. He called the fire back, eliminating any evidence of the flame, besides the charred and melted bodies covering the floor.

"Damn." Mike got to his feet, no longer in his reptilian form.

"Um…" Briar averted her eyes from Mike's nude body. "Wanna cover up?"

"A little help here?" He asked of Jinn. With a wave of a hand, Mike was fully clothed again. "Thanks. Jeans are a little snug, though," he joked.

"How's this?" Jinn lifted his hand and Mike screamed.

"Hey, I was only joking!" The fabric around his crotch loosened again and he sighed with the relief. "Damn, I'd like to have a chance at a son, you know."

"Are you okay, Jinn?" Briar laid her hand on his shoulder, but he flinched away from her touch.

"I'm fine. Let's go." In a moment, he'd gone from humor to anger. Reality reached him as the stench of burned flesh and the rot of mutated blood filled his nostrils.

Traveling back to the exit was a silent, tension filled trek. Again, they stopped to rest up; this time Jinn went straight to sleep, no gifts of fresh food for the locals. Mike and Briar gave him space, time to process his thoughts, and when Cole questioned about food, Mike warned him that it was a bad idea. His people wouldn't be getting another magical feast. They'd come in hopes of rescuing his wife and were leaving empty handed.

"Thanks again, Cole." Mike hugged his old friend. They stood at the exit point, smells of the ocean a great relief from the stale stench of the underground.

"Any time. Thanks for keeping me from getting my ass chomped back there." Cole shook his head. "Hell, hopefully that entire ordeal eradicated the gloamer population for us."

"Anytime, man, you know I need you intact!" Mike smiled. "If you need anything, Cole, let me know."

"Yeah, I will." The round man smiled at Briar and nodded at Jinn.

Both returned his silent farewells before he disappeared beneath the ground again.

"Shall we get going?" Mike turned to Jinn who again nodded. The three grabbed hold of each other and disappeared in a swirl of blue magic.

CHAPTER
FIFTEEN

W hen the smoke cleared, they were standing inside of Jinn's garage, next to his black beauty. He ran his hand across the side of the bike, inspecting it. Of course, it hadn't been touched—if it weren't by his hands, the bike never moved.

"As far as Praia knows, we got in and out clean. No mention of the gloamers, or any of that shit," Jinn instructed.

"My lips are sealed," Mike responded, just happy to hear the voice of the man who'd been silent for far too long.

"Same here." Briar wanted to forget the damn things anyway. If Praia found out about them, she would ask a million and one questions, which would make squashing the memory all but impossible.

The door to the home opened, and the moment they stepped across the threshold, they felt it—panic. Praia's emotions radiated from her, filling the home with an alarming sensation.

"Whoa, what the hell is that?" Mike asked, grabbing his chest.

"It's Praia, she is an Empath, and very advanced. She is upset." Jinn moved further into his home. "Praia?" Jinn called out. Scanning the entrance and the living room just off the foyer, he looked for her, but didn't find her lounging in her usual spot on the oversized sofa.

"Jinn? Help!" Her voice called from the kitchen. The three ran to her to find her standing over Sybella, who was slumped over the table. "Help! I don't know what happened. She was fine, and then—"

"Sybella?" Briar pushed past Jinn and Mike to get to the table. Gently, she lifted the seer's head from the table. Blood leaked from her eyes "What the hell happened?" Briar turned and yelled at Praia. "You were supposed to be watching her!"

"I was. I…" Praia shook. "She was fine!"

"Praia calm down. Tell us what happened," Jinn coaxed the fae with a tranquil tone. If she got any more worked up, her emotions would start to overwhelm them all, and that wasn't going to be good for any of them.

"She asked for tea, and I was making it. She said she needed to check in on Alesea, the queen. She said she felt something wasn't right. She couldn't tell, but she could sense some type of panic. Next thing I know, she fell forward on the table, and blood was coming from her eyes. I tried to help, but nothing worked."

"She tried to see Alesea, and this happened?" Mike frowned. "That can't be good, right? Has anything like this ever happened before?"

"No, it hasn't," Briar answered his question, still examining the seer, before turning to Praia. "Did anything else happen? Anything at all, focus!"

"Yes, um, she mumbled something." Praia shook her head, trying to calm down before responding. She knew as well as Jinn just how dangerous it could be if she didn't get a handle on her emotions.

"What? What did she say?"

"I don't know. It was a name, I think." Praia took a deep breath, refusing to let Briar's anxieties rub off on her. "It was difficult to understand."

"What name?" Jinn questioned again with a soothing tone.

"Um, shit... It sounded like Diego, or Digger, or something."

"Daegal," Jinn spoke the name.

"He's here?" Mike stepped to the djinn who held his fists tight at his sides. "Is that possible?"

"Apparently." The djinn looked at Mike.

"Wait, she was trying to peek in on the queen, right? Not us?" Mike was the one to question the fae girl this time. "Are you sure?"

"She said Alesea specifically."

"Shit, that means..." Mike trailed off as the pieces connected.

"We need to get to Vilar." Briar turned to Mike and Jinn who wore mirroring looks of shock. "Now!"

The blue smoke settled in the city of Vilar which was in a state of panic; there wasn't time for a subtler arrival. Besides, not one person who passed them gave a damn about the misfit gang in the streets. When the smoke cleared, they saw that what they feared was true. Vilar was under attack. The tower that stood at the center was under full lock down. Praia joined them this time, after Briar placed a protection spell around the seer only another fairy would be able to cross it. She would send help for the woman who, though she was still unconscious, was stable and had stopped bleeding.

"How are we going to get in?" Mike stared up at the building that was usually transparent with its large glass windows but was now sealed in metal shutters that slid down from the top, locking everything out.

"They will let me inside, I'm the second." Briar ran forward, and as she did, without so much as a word from her, the doors opened. They allowed only her and those she approved to enter the fortress before the building was sealed shut yet again. "Update," Briar barked at the small girl who opened the door.

"The queen is trapped inside the chamber." Her voice trembled with the weight of her fear and sorrow. She, like so many others, had already accepted the worst. "We cannot get the doors open. Mysti says she can feel another within."

"Why haven't we gone in?" Briar asked, confused by their lack of action. She forged ahead with the small girl shuffling along beside her, and Jinn, Praia, and Mike followed close behind. "There are other ways inside that room!"

"Any time anyone gets close, they die." The girl stumbled along. "We've tried every entrance. No one has gotten through alive."

"What?" Briar paused momentarily, giving the girl a chance to explain. "We've lost people?"

"Yes, there is a perimeter set up. It looks like anything within ten feet of the door. At least that is as close as anyone has managed to get." She paused, throwing a glance at Mike, and scrunching her nose. "Why is he here?"

"Does that seem like an appropriate question to ask me right now?" Briar snapped with an authority that caused the girl to frown and drop her head with an apology. "Any plans for getting around this perimeter?" She continued marching forward to the queen's chamber, and the four of them followed suit.

"No. Unfortunately, nothing we have tried has worked," she repeated herself. "Mysti is heading up the team working to find a way inside."

"Shit. Okay, we're going up. Mike, stay down here please, just in case we need more muscle power." She turned to the small girl again.

"Get one of the healers to Sybella, now. She is hurt in Jinn's home." The girl nodded and ran off. "Jinn, Praia, come with me."

"Are you sure you want me down here? Doesn't feel at all welcoming," Mike asked before he was left alone. Just a few feet away were a group of fairy guards, all of whom looked at the man like he was enemy number one.

Bria responded in a tone that resonated throughout the large space, echoing back to them, "You are here to help us, you arrived by my side. No one here will question that, or else they would be questioning my judgement." She laid eyes on the fairies who watched them. They all nodded, a show of respect. They may not like Mike, but they would do him no harm.

"Okay, well, thanks." Mike was in definite awe of the power Briar possessed; it was no wonder she was second in command.

The group left Mike by himself, uncomfortably positioned with the fairies. The elevator shot to the top of the crown where Mysti, a fairy with an air affinity, stood at the head of a group of guards—with a frantic, yet strategic focus, as they tried to find a way into the queen's chamber.

"Mysti," Briar addressed the head fairy as she stepped from the elevator, "report."

"Briar, thank the heavens, you are back!" Mysti quickly moved away from the others to Briar's side. "We can't get in. I've even tried to use the air to force my way inside, but as soon as it hits that boundary, it goes no further." Mysti was dressed the same as the others—black head to toe—but her hair hung around her face in blue waves. Their leader's style had become popular for combat. Outside of the job, she dressed as elaborately as all the other fairies. She glanced briefly at Briar's companions but knew better than to question their attendance.

"And what about the others, same result?" Briar continued, making note of who was in the room. There were two of the front line that were missing.

"Yes, unfortunately." Mysti shook her head.

"Shit, have we tried entering from the back passage?" There was a secret passage that lead to the chambers. Not many knew about it, but all of the top-level guards were well aware. It was to be used in cases of emergency, such as the one they were in.

"Yes, same scenario. We even tried coming from above. We lost Fia and Rig." Mysti confirmed Briar's suspicion with the names of the two who weren't in line.

"Damn it!" Briar looked at the team. Panic was beginning to consume them, she had to keep them all levelheaded. Her mind raced, trying to find a way to penetrate the field that held their queen hostage.

"This can't be right," Praia stated in a low tone, having been drawn to the perimeter of the magical field. "How?"

"What is it?" Jinn left Briar who was deep in thought and

calculating her next move.

"This magic, it's fae," Praia whispered, not wanting to alarm anyone. If they thought the magic was fae, they might assume her people were making a move against them. That wasn't the case, she knew it, but they wouldn't.

"What?" He whispered back, she was keeping her claim hushed, and Jinn quickly caught on as to why.

"It's moon energy." She stepped forward, holding her hand out, and coming dangerously close to the boundary marked on the floor.

"Praia, stop!" Jinn called out, his fear that she was wrong crippled his ability to stop her.

She leaned forward, reaching further until her fingers touch the boundary, but she was unharmed. From the tips of her finger, streams of cream-colored light shot out in all directions, as the magic of the moon recognized its child.

"How is this possible? How is he using fae magic?" She turned to Jinn with a worried gaze.

"I don't know, but right now you're our only hope of getting in there and stopping whatever the hell he is about to do." Briar appeared by the djinn's side, hope flushing over her for the first time since she'd come home.

Praia nodded, understanding what Briar wanted, and without question moved toward the door. The shield opened just enough for her singular form to pass through. Carefully, she moved forward, not wanting to alert whoever was inside to her presence. As her hand touched the large gold knob, a gut-curdling scream rang out. Praia looked back to the group of fairies, all with horrified expressions. The scream was from Alesea—their queen was hurt. She turned the knob, but paused again when she noticed, beneath the view of her hand, crimson flowing from under the door. "Oh, no," she whispered, but before she could enter the room to confirm her fears, Briar doubled over with sobs.

"She's dead!" She cried out.

Jinn rushed forward, past Praia. The magic barrier had dropped, giving him access to the space and further confirming what they all knew to be true. He pushed the door open. In the dark of the room, he smelled her first, the sweet scent of fairy blood, the quick release of the magic of the queen as it escaped her lifeless form and flowed like a river, tried and true, to the next in line to take the throne. He conjured light, setting flame to the sconces lining the walls of the room. In the blue light of his magic, he laid eyes upon the crumpled body of Alesea. Her hands were covered in the blood that leaked from the opening on her torso. Her eyes were wide and blank with death as the color faded from her skin, leaving her once honey tone in the deathly shade of gray.

He exited the room, looking around the hall at the late queen's constituents. "She is gone." Cries rang out as the fairies mourned their queen. Throughout the city of Vilar, the anguish was heard.

People stopped in the streets, exited their home, all to stare at the sky and sob. Jinn focused on Briar who sat on her knees, silent. He took two steps toward her but stopped. The light of the queen, the magic that seeped from Alesea, traveled in a visible string of golden energy, from within the chamber, past the fae who still stood by the entrance, and to Briar. She opened her arms, baring her chest to the force, and accepted her rightful place as their new queen.

CHAPTER
SIXTEEN

"**Y**ou're the queen now?" Mike stood in the now empty hall with the others. The room had been cleared; the former queen's body taken so that it may be prepared for her return to the sun.

"It would seem." Briar nodded, her face still damp from the tears she shed. This was not something she wanted; Alesea was a good queen to their people. "Well before my time."

"Shit." He shook his head. "I'm sorry."

Briar nodded again, this time with a small smile before her face turned hard again, burying her emotions. "There is a problem."

"What is it?" Praia asked. She was having a hard time being in Vilar with all the fairies' emotions. She tried her best to drown out the feelings, but every single soul in the city was mourning, and it stretched out further as the news traveled to other locations.

"The Solaris stone, it's gone." She kept her voice low; only a select few knew of its absence, and to alert any others would cause a panic that would wreak havoc upon the city.

"What stone?" Mike asked and looked to the others who seemed more informed, but not entirely.

"Come with me." Briar led them back to the chamber, pausing just before stepping inside, the scent of blood, though cleaned from the surface of the floor, still lingered beneath the smell of cleaning solutions. She walked over to the throne, where she and every queen before her was meant to sit. Just above the headrest, was an opening. "Right here," she pointed to the space which upon closer look had been damaged, "this is where it's meant to be, the Solaris stone. It is meant to harness the power of the sun. It concentrates it, allowing us to remain connected to its power even when it's not above. It is also how we all stay connected, as one. Without it, our people are vulnerable. In time, the connection will begin to fade." She looked to the three who had become her friends, her partners—she needed their help. "We must find it, before it's too late."

"Guys…" Praia stumbled back, holding her chest. Her eyes fell on Jinn, pain filled the wide orbs just as it painted her voice. "I need to call home."

"Yes, okay." Jinn conjured a portal, his version of a cellular phone. It allowed the user to peek in on anyone, anywhere. Because the portal was meant for her, Praia was the only one who could see the other side.

Praia peered through, her eyes frantically scanning a scene of chaos. She clutched her chest and shook her head. Tears, from her own sorrow, poured freely from reddened eyes. "This can't be."

"What's wrong?" Mike spoke softly to her. Jinn taught him quickly how to deal with her. He needed to remember that she was an Empath and do nothing to further upset her.

"My home, it was attacked as well. The Lunaire stone, it works the same as the Solaris, it was stolen."

"This cannot be good. Both stones taken on the same night." Mike turned to Jinn. "Briar was right. She said we would know when he started in on his plan. This makes a huge statement. He attacked two of the most powerful houses."

"Is your king okay?" Jinn, more concerned with Praia, put his arm around her.

Praia nodded, her head low. "He is badly injured, but alive. His son was trapped with him. The prince has been lost."

"Shit," Mike muttered. "I'm so sorry, Praia." Before he could stop himself, he pulled the girl away from Jinn and into his arms, and she sobbed.

"Why would he take them both? We have to figure out what his end game is. Where is this leading?" Briar directed her comment to

Jinn. She felt just as much as the others, but as the new queen, she didn't have the time or space for mourning—that would come later, after she had solved their problems.

"He has essentially crippled two of the most powerful forces that exist today." The djinn paced the floor. "It seems like a plot for something more. With the fae and the fairies down, who else is there to stop him?"

"He also still has a collection of djinns to make his every wish come true," Mike reminded them. He hadn't brought up Nitara specifically, but it made no difference. Jinn's jaw tightened even further.

"Something tells me we're going to need a lot more help." Mike, the only one not suffering from immediate heartache, helped Praia to a nearby seat. She was hurting more than the others knew and he had a very good idea of why. That would have to wait for a later conversation.

"Praia, can you get your people word about what's happening here? Recruit whatever help you can. Mike—" Briar turned to him but was cut off by the slither who shook his head.

"Sorry." Mike held up his hands, stopping Briar from continuing. "I hate to break it to you, but my people aren't going to be jumping up to volunteer for this gig."

"What?" The new queen lifted her chin just slightly, taking offense to his statement.

"I can speak for most in saying, as far as they are concerned, the empire can fall." Mike was blunt in his response. His people wouldn't care about what was going on in Vilar and she needed to know the complete truth.

"How can you say that?"

"Come on, you've seen with your own eyes what my people live like, what they are subjected to day in and day out. Living in dark tunnels, running from monsters who want them as a meal. Your people insured that we have to live that way, and hell, I've seen worse. Now you want them to jump up and help you protect all of this?" He laughed because as ridiculous as it sounded, he actually had to spell it out for her. "Then what happens? Do they get to go crawl back into their tunnels while you and your people resume the life of peaceful luxury? Sorry, but you're going to have to come with something way better than a few pleases and thank yous."

"What do you want?" Briar lowered her guard, thinking about what Mike said. He was right—those families, those children, lived in the worst possible conditions. Who was she to ask that they defend that way of life? They had nothing worth fighting for.

"We want better living, a place to call our own that isn't the slums of the earth, the scorched lands where no one else desires to live." He paused, knowing that the topic often got him riled up. This wasn't the time for letting his emotions get the best of him. "Every other species, including the trolls, as horrible as they are, have their place. They have a sanctuary where they know they are safe; they can live their lives without worry of being hunted or murdered. Their children are safe and in healthy homes. This is what we want, it is what we have always wanted."

"And if I can make that happen?" She stepped forward. She wanted to help, from the moment she saw the child in the tunnel, she wanted to free her of that world.

"Then you will have our help." Mike mirrored her action, taking a step closer to close the gap between them.

"How can you promise that?" Briar looked him in the eyes, searching for even a hint of dishonesty. "How can you speak for the rest? Am I simply to take your word?"

"He is their king," Jinn offered, an attempt to avoid any unnecessary tension, or disrespect. Mike took a lot from Briar, but he shouldn't have. Yes, he was the king of the slithers, the unwanted, but that still counted for something.

"What?" Praia stood from her seat, suddenly interested in the conversation again. "You're a king?" She wiped away tears, sniffling.

"Born of the first, and one of the only ones who has a chance of blending in with normal society, yeah. It was more of a process of elimination."

"I never knew. I..." Briar stepped back from him, a show of respect for his status.

"Look, no need to treat me any different than before you heard that. I'm just a spokesperson, because no one else can be. We know there were some people who did shady shit in the past. Unfortunately, those acts were taken as a standard, an example of who and what we are. We're just asking that not all of us be punished for the acts of a few."

"We will help your people, if you agree to help us." Briar understood wholeheartedly what Mike, the expecting father, meant.

"Well, it looks like we have a deal." Mike smiled and clapped his hands. "All right. I could use a drink, anyone else?"

CHAPTER
SEVENTEEN

Mike walked forward across the damaged earth, followed by Briar and two of her guards. Her visit to the scorched lands to speak with his people was a necessity. It was a show of solidarity. No other fairy queen had come there before; her appearance showed that she was truly trying to take a step in the right direction. The council, a collective of slithers who aided Mike in leading their people, would need a lot more than his word.

Briar brought two fairies with her. The new queen of her people, she would never be allowed to go into what was considered enemy territory without back up. Especially with what had just occurred to their former queen. With her was Mysti, her new second, and another fairy named Boxi. She was the largest fairy guard; her affinity for Earth was a primary reason for her size. They often joked that it was the act of moving Earth that made her so muscular, though none of the others were nearly as big.

"Are you sure about this?" Briar paused; they weren't far from the general population. She could hear the sounds of life, surprisingly cheerful for the conditions in which they lived. If there were any doubts at all, then this was the time to voice them.

"Yes, you're coming here as my guest. Regardless of their personal issues, they will respect my wishes and hear you out. As long as you don't have a plan to go back on your word."

"My word is my bond. You and your people will be taken care of," Briar asserted. Nothing was more important to her people than their word. It was their honor, their respect—once lost, it could never be regained.

"Good, because we're here." He pointed, leading their attention where just ahead of them, below the hill, was the scorched lands— earth burned by fires and poisoned by chemical warfare. It was where the worst of the damage had occurred, but in the midst of the death and the destruction, there was life. Mike's people were left there … children, families, living lives as best they could considering their current conditions.

"I had no idea it was this bad out here," Boxi whispered as though the people down below would hear her and take offense to her words.

"You, like everyone else who is a part of your world, chose not to consider it. And that's okay. We have a tendency to take care of our own, which is exactly what I am doing now." Mike was kind in his reply. He didn't blame her or any of the fairies. It had been done, the goal was to undo it, not to point blame.

"Are you sure you want to go in there?" Mysti questioned Briar. "What if they aren't as welcoming as you hope?"

"Yes. This is a time of change, for everyone." Briar nodded. "I can take a little hate if it starts us in the right direction."

They continued on, walking, following just a few paces behind Mike. Briar didn't want his people to think she was there for anything other than to make peace. She kept a calm demeanor, smiling and making reassuring eye contact with whoever would dare to look at her. As they reached the population of the scorch lands, all eyes were transfixed on the visitors. There were murmurs, hisses, and growls, but no one approached. No one said anything or showed any form of outrage or disrespect for the visitors. They respected Mike as their king. Briar struggled to keep her smile and hold back tears as she witnessed children in tattered clothing, babies who were malnourished, frail, and sickly. With each face, her heart broke even more. They lived in huts built from reclaimed materials scavenged from places where no one dwelled; abandoned neighborhoods like the one Jinn lived in. Most of their homes left them exposed to the elements, the structures barely qualified as shelter. Briar's heart was heavier than it had ever been. These people didn't deserve to live in such terrible conditions. Their children had done nothing wrong, and yet they lived as if they had committed the worst crimes. The fairies, and every other entity of power, blamed the humans for all that went wrong with the world. Humans were cast aside for being evil, so wicked that they would turn against their own, and yet here they were, no better—allowing generations of supernatural beings, just like them, to live in squalor.

"Something must be done," she whispered to herself.

"Well, you can do something, now," Mike responded, though her words were not for him. He paused outside of a stacked group of old shipping containers, fashioned together to create the town center. "Are you ready?"

"Right." The new queen straightened. "Yes, I will do something. I'm ready."

Mike opened the heavy metal door, revealing the inside of the containers. Rusted and worn, holes formed in the sides of the make shift building by a process of natural degrading and added light to the room. The effect almost seemed intentional if not for the candles that were lit as well. Mike entered first, and Briar followed with Mysti at her side. Boxi remained outside for security; if this was an attempt to attack their new queen, she would move the Earth before letting them succeed.

The murmurs started the moment she stepped inside the space, and Mike waited patiently for the group to come to attention. He knew her presence would do anything but put them at ease, which was why he'd sent word ahead of their expected guests. The grumbles subsided quickly as Mike lifted his hand and called for their attention. "I ask that you all listen to what Briar has to say. She is the new Fairy Queen, and as the leader of her people she comes here, offering us help, in exchange for our assistance."

"Our assistance? So she's here to bribe us?" A brute older man sat at the far end of a table crafted from old wood and metal. His face was lined with a thick coat of grey hair that would have been three shades lighter if he had ready access to clean water.

"Relk, please, hold your comments for later. Let's hear what the girl has to say." Two seats over from the burly man was a slender woman whose features told that she was of a younger generation. Trex was one who couldn't shed her reptilian side, not entirely. Though her face, half shadowed by the low light, appeared normal, a prominent lizard tail laid on the ground at her feet.

Mike gave her the floor. "Briar."

"I must first apologize to you all." She looked around the room, taking in the stern faces of the seven council members. This was not going to be an easy feat. "I, like so many others, have simply forgotten about you. All of you out here, victims of a war that was not your own. Our people have not done enough to rectify what has been done to you. It is easy, living as we do, to forget those who are less fortunate, much too easy. I had no idea that this was the lives you and your families led. And until fighting side by side with your leader," she nodded at Mike, who returned the show of respect, "living for just one day as you all do every day, there was no way I could ever really understand it.

"Nothing I say or do here will fix the past, it won't change the fact that you have spent decades suffering for the acts of a few. I'm not here to erase the past. That is something that simply cannot be done. I am here offering to you, all of you, a better future. Should you choose to help us or not." Mysti scoffed and Briar shot her a look that told her to back down. If she didn't agree with her decision, that was something to speak to her about in private. It was not a matter of debate, and definitely not in front of outsiders. "Yes, our people need your help, and if what we are facing is as terrible as we believe it is, your people are at risk as well. If you choose not to help, I will understand your positioning. I do, however, hope that you choose in the best way for your own people, as our queen before me did for ours."

"You would help us, without bargain?" the woman spoke again, leaning into the light to reveal the scaled side of her face previously hidden in the shadows.

"Yes. Those children, those babies, they don't deserve this." Briar shook her head. "I don't believe that any of you deserve to live like this."

The council members looked to one another, passing concerned and questioning gazes across the table. None of them wanted to discuss the issue further, not with Briar in the room. Though she came there in what seemed to be good faith, they still did not trust her or her kind.

Mike reclaimed the floor from Briar. "Give us time to discuss."

Complying, Briar and Mysti made their exit, leaving him behind to discuss the matters at hand with the skeptical council.

"How did it go?" Boxi questioned, relieved that the two appeared without any sign of concern.

"We'll find out soon. They're discussing matters now," Mysti answered her as Briar was too preoccupied with a small girl who walked by. The child was covered in filth, limping from an injury, and still she smiled brightly at her friends just a few feet ahead. When she reached them, her soft giggle fluttered over to Briar who couldn't help but smile. There was still hope and it was inside of that little girl. Even if the prior generations could never forgive what was done, they would do what was right for their children, she knew it.

Mike emerged from the door with a smile on his face. "It appears we have a deal."

"They have agreed to help us?" Briar asked. She'd been worried that they might accept her offer of aide without any return responsibility on their end.

"I simply explained to them that what you are up against will negatively affect us as the threat comes from the Ashen." He smiled. "That alone was enough. We aren't exactly thrilled with the current powers that be, but to have some ancient warlock from the darkest part of the coven take over things ... well, we all agree that we must do whatever is necessary to prevent that from happening."

"That's good news." Briar smiled, trying not to give too much of a show of her relief. "What's next? Is there anything you need me to do now?"

"Next, you go back home, and I get my people together. If you need to reach me, Jinn knows how," Mike said. "Oh, and I promised them you would be sending food and fresh water here."

"Right, yes, we will get on that." Briar turned to Mysti. "Please put in the call. Have supplies brought by air." She paused, turning to Mike. "Is it okay for air supplies? I wouldn't want to alarm anyone." Not everyone knew of the deal they'd just struck; fairies taking flight above them might prove disarming, especially because it wasn't an area they ever came near.

"Yes, I will make sure everyone knows what to expect." Mike indicated the men leaving out of the side of the council chambers. "They are spreading the word as we speak."

"Great. Mysti, please get that going." Briar nodded again.

"We're just supposed to walk back out of here?" Boxi asked, obviously getting anxious being in the scorch lands. The place was toxic, there was no telling how the environment there would affect them if they stayed for too long. Mysti kept the air circulating around them as best as she could, but in time, that too wouldn't be enough.

"Yes, no one will bother you. As I said, news is spreading as we speak about your generous offer," Mike stated with a wide smile. "Besides, you walked in with me, and you will leave without issue. The perks of being something of a king."

"When do you plan on returning?" Though Boxi was eager to leave, Briar still had questions.

"When things are arranged here. There will be a lot to do." Mike waved at a group of children, one of whom was the girl that brought a smile to Briar's face. They called his name and then ran away giggling. "The council will help to arrange things, but we have to spread the word to everyone. There are groups of slithers all over the world. They need to hear this news from me directly, and that will take some time to get done. At least a few days."

"Do you need any assistance with that?" she offered, knowing that kind of travel would be easier with a bit of fairy magic.

"No. Trust me, we have our ways."

"Great. You can expect the supply drop in the next few hours." Mysti rejoined the conversation after calling back to Vilar. "Are we good to go?"

"Yes, there is much to be done." The three fairies walked out of the scorched lands, just far enough away from those who lived there. Once out of the marked boundaries, they took flight, their fairy wings carrying them back to Vilar.

⁊⌡⁊

"We need to find out where he is." Briar sat in the small room that was set just off to the right of the chamber room with Jinn. There they could sit together and speak in private. The room was a simple space, with a long wood table, stained a deep shade of burgundy. They sat together at one end of the table, leaving the other eighteen chairs empty. Briar preferred the space to the chamber room, which still reminded her of the death of her friend and former queen, and the loss of the Solaris stone.

"How do you suggest we do that?" Jinn sat back in his chair, running his fingers through his hair. "We have no way of tracking him. Hell, we don't even know what this guy looks like. He may no longer have the appearance I remember."

"I tried Sybella, but the seer was unable to help us. She is hurt really bad. The healers say she may take a long time to recover, and if she does, she may not ever be fully restored." Briar sighed as she thought about the mental state of the woman she'd visited when she returned from the scorched lands. Sybella was held up in her room, mumbling to herself about evil.

"What's our alternative?" He lifted the beer to his lips, having opted out of the sweet wine that was originally offered to him.

"Tracker spell?" Briar tossed out the idea already knowing it was futile.

"Not without something of his," he replied, confirming what she already knew.

"Well, considering his home was sent up in flames, I say that is highly unlikely." She laughed dryly. "Talk about a stroke of bad luck!"

"What if we could use me for the spell?" Jinn pepped up.

"You?"

"His magic is what created me. It was a long time ago, but perhaps there is still enough there, some signature that we can use." It was the only thing they had, and even it was a slim chance.

"It's worth a shot." Briar pressed a small button on the arm of her chair that summoned her second in command, Mysti. When the fairy entered the room Briar issued her request. "Please go retrieve Rebecca. Tell her that we need her assistance."

"Rebecca?" Jinn watched Mysti closely as she left the room to carry out the order. He'd had an odd feeling about the woman since they met, and it wasn't going away.

"She's a witch, one of the few on our side. She's the only one I know that is capable of tracing magical signatures." She paused, considering the man at her side. They hadn't discussed how he was doing with everything. From the moment they returned, they were on a race to find Daegal, and Jinn's concerns had taken a backseat to the chaos. "Are you okay?"

"I'm managing." He straightened in his seat, not ready for the conversation that was about to happen. He'd been happy for the distractions that arose when they returned from the Collective.

Briar tilted her head. "I'm worried about you, Jinn. I know this is hard on you."

"Yes, you're right. It is difficult for me right now. The thing is, there is nothing I can do about that."

"When we were in the Ashen, your anger, I've never seen you that way before." They weren't the best of friends, but they'd known each other. Jinn visited sparingly Vilar as he was a tolerated guest, and most times he was there she'd see him. It wasn't long until he figured out that their accidental encounters were planned. She had to keep an eye on the powerful outsider no matter how accepted his presence was. In all the time, she'd never seem him display any emotion besides a casual show of aloofness.

"It's been quite some time since I've had reason to be that angry."

"Right." She paused, considering her next words carefully. "Do you think you can contain it?"

Before he could answer, the door opened and in walked Mysti followed by a short, chubby woman who smelled of whisky and mint. The odor filled the room quickly. Jinn raised a questioning eyebrow at Briar who shook her head. This couldn't be the person she wanted to help them. Rebecca had become more liberal with the spirits in the past few years. Briar knew it was because of the things the woman had seen. Most often when she was asked to use her gift, it was to track someone or something that was horrible, their magic dark. The woman wore a crooked smile as she was escorted inside of the room by Mysti.

"Are you sure she is up to this?" Jinn questioned as the woman stumbled over to the chair Mysti directed her to and plopped down into it.

"Yes, sorry, she has taken Alesea's death really hard. They were close." Briar left out the rest of the reasoning for Rebecca's condition.

"Briar," Rebecca hiccupped. "Ooh, my apologies." She covered her mouth and giggled. "I am at your services." Glossed-over eyes found the new queen at the opposite end of the table.

"Rebecca, we need you to perform a tracking spell, do you think you can do that for us?" Briar kept her tone soft, coaxing. The witch was on edge, had been for a while, but even more so with the death of her friend.

"Well, of course I can!" she shouted, pointing her finger to the ceiling as she stood from the chair. She stepped away from the table, but her momentum continued, and she stumbled backwards into Mysti's arms. Once back to her feet she asked, "Who would you like to have tracked?"

"A warlock," Jinn answered. "His name is Daegal."

The woman's expression sobered up quickly. The rosy color caused by the whiskey drained from her cheeks. "Oh, no, no, no, I cannot. Oh no." She shook her head. "He is … oh no, nope. I just can't." She slid back into her designated chair.

"Rebecca, we need your help." Briar kept an even tone, realizing the fragile state of the woman's mind.

"Oh, I'm sure you do, but," she paused for a belch that turned into a hiccup, "you don't know what it is that you're asking of me. I'm afraid that is out of my doing."

"Is it really?" Jinn stepped in, challenging her.

"Well, I—" she began. She was bluffing and he called her on it, no one ever had before.

"You what?" again he challenged, and they waited to see if the woman would in fact fall apart.

"He is evil, the darkest of magic I've ever heard of. If I try to track him, he will know it, and he will come after me. I just can't do it." She shook with fear.

"Rebecca, we will protect you." Briar leaned forward in her chair. "You have to know that."

"Like you protected Alesea?" She couldn't stop the words from passing her lips. She slapped her hands over her mouth. "Oh, Briar, I am so sorry!"

"It is okay." Briar stood from her seat to walk over to Rebecca's side. She wrapped her arms around the woman, warming her with her magic. It would ease her pain. "I understand, and you are in no way obligated to help us with this."

"I really wish that I could." She looked up at the woman who held her. "I do, but I don't want him to come after me. I don't want him to do what he's done to so many others."

"Rebecca, please do not worry." She helped the woman up from her seat. "You should go get yourself some rest." With an understanding smile, she handed Rebecca off to Mysti, who walked her to the exit and gave instructions for another fairy to make sure she made it home safely.

"Great, now what are we going to do?" Mysti returned to the table. "Is there a plan B?"

"We're going to track him," Jinn spoke.

"With no witch?" She laughed. "How exactly do you plan to do that?"

"I'm a witch, or at least I used to be. I'll track him. There has to be a way." He frowned. He couldn't give up, not that easily, not because a witch was too drunk and afraid to help. "There must be some sort of connection between us. If I can find it, I can use it to tell us where he is."

"Are you sure you can do it?" Briar had made her way back to her seat and to the glass of wine she'd been nursing since she'd joined Jinn in the room.

"No, I'm not entirely sure, but it should be simple enough to accomplish." Jinn thought back to a time before he was turned into a djinn, when the magic of his ancestors came to him like second nature. That was changed when he was. Though he could still feel it there, he had been disconnected from it. He never attempted to repair that connection, unsure what it would do to him. In this case, he really didn't have any other choice.

"What if what Rebecca says is true? What if he will be able to tell that you're tracking him?" Mysti still stood at the end of the table, never being asked to leave the room.

"Then he'll know I'm coming for him." Jinn stood from his seat, no longer wanting to remain in the space. Unlike the witch who'd stumbled out of the room sobbing, he wasn't afraid to face Daegal. Hell, he'd been waiting for centuries for a chance.

CHAPTER
EIGHTEEN

Praia positioned herself across from Jinn. It was the first time she'd been allowed to witness him as he meditated. It had always been a private event for the man, so when he asked her to be there, she jumped on the chance. It also concerned her—if he wanted her there, it meant that this wasn't going to be a normal session and she may need to intervene. He sat on the floor across from her and eased himself into a deeper level of consciousness. His legs were folded, and his hands posed atop each knee with fingers pointed towards the sky. A soft blue light danced across his fingertips and his eyelids fluttered. He asked her to act as his anchor while he did what he needed to do to find a connection to Daegal. It would take a lot out of him to reconnect with his magic and then use it to repair and follow the broken link back to the warlock responsible for its disconnection.

Briar had allowed them to use the chamber; she didn't want to be there, so any excuse not to occupy the space was good enough for her. It was the one place where they could be sure they wouldn't be interrupted by the guards or anyone else who might be looking for the new queen. The room had been spelled by the fairies to provide privacy and protection. Jinn also thought it would be easier to connect with Daegal because he had been in the space, or at least his magic had. He could use those traces left behind to enhance the link between them. He hoped like hell that he wasn't barking up the wrong tree because it looked like the last one in the field.

In order to connect to Daegal, to find the link between them, Jinn had to strip away all of his barriers. He had to drop all of the walls he'd worked to put in place for centuries and go back to a time he wanted nothing more than to forget.

He'd done all he could to save the village, using natural elements to work to repair the damage that had been done. He used air, stripping it from areas long enough to suffocate the flames that threatened to burn the village to the ground. He used water to wash away the evidence of blood. The ground was tossed, hiding the damage. He worked through the town, doing all that he could, against the wishes of his wife. Two weeks had gone by and the small village was still under attack. Those who hadn't either fled, or already died, were terrified. They came to him, requesting his help, and he didn't have it in him to turn them away. He was always too late when he made it to them. Each time he arrived, the threat was gone, having left the town devastated once again and its occupants feeling hollow.

It was a late night when his mind wouldn't settle. He stepped outside of his home to stare at the blanket of the night sky, which was the darkest he had ever seen it. Nitara had long since gone to bed, the sunset having passed and the moon strangely not within view. It took a while before he realized that the sky was not the still portrait he was used to, it was moving ... liquid darkness shadowing out the world. His breath caught in his chest as his eyes followed the flow of the darkness off into the distance. It spilled down to the surface of the earth, just above the village. He couldn't help himself. He took off running, hoping that he could make it in time to help. As he neared the small village, the sounds of screams reached his ears. The people, the few who dared to remain, were being tortured.

He slowed his pace as he neared the village border, not knowing what he was running into; he had to take the time to really assess the situation. The outskirts had long since been abandoned. The charred homes no longer provided shelter for families. As he got closer to the center of the village where the market was held, he witnessed more damage, more destruction. Buildings had collapsed in on themselves. Granted they weren't modern day structures built with metal and reinforced, but the homes were made strong, using brick and wood. They'd survived torrential downpours, some of the worst storms imaginable, but not the havoc caused by this new plague. As he neared, walking carefully, he heard the whimpers of a small child, someone unable to fend for themselves. Jinn picked up his pace, he remained careful in his movement, but urgently tried to get to the source of the cries.

Sitting on the pedestal where the town crier would stand to relay important information from other places, was a small child. She was covered in soot, her dark hair matted to her skin heavy with dirt and sweat. Tears made streaks down her face in the ash that covered her flesh. He ran to her, kneeling down to find the face of the girl. She looked up to him and sobbed. Everything she'd known had been taken away, the fear in her eyes was heartbreaking.

"Jinn." She recognized him as someone who would help her, and for a brief second there was relief in her eyes.

"Annabelle, what are you doing out here alone?" Jinn knew the girl, he often chatted with her while her mother shopped at the market. The small girl was intrigued with cows and their milk. Every time she came, she had more questions to ask him. He loved indulging her and told her that she could come visit his farm whenever she wanted. She never did get a chance to make that visit.

"They are all gone. He took them all." She looked up to him as if still trying to figure out how to process everything that had happened.

"Who?" He knelt to get closer to her face. "Who took them?"

"The man in the shadows." She sobbed, rocking herself. "I can't find my brother; he was to stay with me. Papa is going to be so upset."

"We will find him, together, okay?" He held out his hand for her to grab. Her small hand wrapped as far as it could around his fingers, and he helped her to her feet. "Where did you last see him?"

"I don't know. We were running, like the others, running to get away. Everything was on fire, all of the buildings. All of the food was lost." She sniffled, turning to look around them at nothing in particular. "He was holding my hand, but then he wasn't. I don't remember letting him go! I stopped running and tried to find him, but I couldn't. Everyone else was gone, they all vanished. I'm all alone now, aren't I?"

Large, dark eyes peered up at the witch who had no answer for her. He thought about scooping the girl up and running out of town. She could live with them. They would never replace her family, but Nitara would be a great caregiver to the girl.

"Keep your thoughts positive, no matter what. There is always a chance to save the person you love. Okay?" He put on his best smile and pulled a handkerchief from his pocket. With slow wipes, as not to get any of the ash in her eyes, he cleaned her face.

She nodded and wrapped her arms around his waist, hugging him. "Thank you."

"We need to get you to safety, and then I will look for your brother, okay?"

Reluctantly the girl nodded and accepted his plan. "I want to help, but I'm tired. I need to find my brother." She coughed. "My chest, it burns." She held one hand over her burning chest, and the other over her cramping stomach. Jinn had to get her out of there, she had inhaled too much smoke and he knew it would be causing her a ton of pain. Jinn scouted the area for the quickest way to safety. All possible exit points were blocked, except the way he'd come. As he viewed the area, he realized he'd fallen for an obvious trick that he should have seen coming. He'd walked straight into a trap. Lifting Annabelle into his arms, he made a dash for it, but he was far too late. The path lit up in a blaze. The flames were as dark as night, but hotter than anything he'd ever felt before.

He turned, scanning for other options, there were none. He had to remain calm, if for nothing other than reassuring the girl in his arms that she would be okay. He would keep her safe.

The sky lit up above them with a lightning show. Jinn looked up, thinking how Nitara would love the view. He used the flashes of light to help him survey the area. A few steps ahead, there was a small space, just wide enough for him to fit through. However, when he ran for it, the dark river that inhabited the sky spilled down in front of him.

"No," Annabelle whispered. "That's him, the man of the shadows."

As the form expanded, a cloud of dark smoke reached out to them. Jinn backed up and tightened his hold on the girl.

"What the hell do you want with these people?" Jinn stood in front of the man cloaked in darkness. His features were hidden behind the veil.

"I want nothing from them." He leaned forward, pushing through the darkness, and revealed his pale face, yellowed teeth, and gray eyes. The warlock who reeked of death and the dark power that he'd invited into himself, smiled a wide grin that seemed too big for his face. "It took you long enough. I thought I had pegged you all wrong. Not very many of them left alive. Was afraid you didn't actually care about them."

"What?" He glanced to the girl and back to the shadows. "You can't have her!"

"Oh, I do not want her," the deep voice laughed. "The girl is of no use to me. It is you that I want!"

"Me?" His heart stopped as the girl in his arms vanished into thin air. She was nothing but a mirage, bait to get him within the warlock's grasp. Shackles lifted from the ground below him, grabbing hold of his arms and pulling him down to his knees. They pinned him in place. Jinn struggled against the magic that held him down but couldn't get free. He'd walked into a trap. The warlock wanted him. He could think of only Nitara. She told him not to help but he did, and because of it, he might lose her forever.

"Yes," the shadowed man moved in closer, and a long, frail finger reached out to Jinn, "you." He tapped the man on the forehead. The power that sparked from just his fingertip was enough to send Jinn flying backwards where he landed in the dirt. His head smacked the ground, causing the world to shift in and out of focus and make him nauseous. Though he had little sense of where he was, Jinn managed to lift his hands just in time, using the powerful force of air to break free of his shackles and block the next attack.

"Who are you?" Jinn cried out.

"Oh, I am your worst nightmare, however cliché it may sound." The warlock laughed a hollowed sound that echoed through the empty village. "Well, you certainly are a strong one. Very good, indeed. It means my efforts to find you have not been in vain."

"What the hell do you want?" He struggled to maintain his shield and looked for a way out.

"You, or rather your potential. There aren't many witches like you, vessels of such great power, and yet you sit here and deny what you were meant to be." He launched another attack, which Jinn blocked, and it made him giggle with joy. "Oh, yes, yes. I like you. You will make a fine addition to my collection."

"Collection?" Jinn needed to keep the man talking, he would

find a way out. There had to be one. Just keep him talking until there was room to bolt. He made it to his feet, no longer seasick from the blow. From the corner of his eye he saw it, the exit he sought, the break in the fire. He would only need a second to run for it, just a moment to break away.

"Hush now, no more questions, come, come." Daegal tossed out a lasso of green light, ready to contain Jinn, but he missed when Jinn sidestepped the shot. The mistake was just the distraction he needed. Jinn rolled out of the way and shot a blanket of air at the warlock. The air obeyed his command, pinning the shadow man to the ground long enough for him to make his escape. "You won't get far!" the man called behind him. "I've marked you; you belong to me now!"

Jinn ran through the woods, forcing his limbs to move as fast as he could. His magic aided him, making his legs feel lighter as he powered forward. His mind was heavy, though; he knew what he had to do. He would have to break Nitara's heart and pull her from the life they'd built together. The best thing about his girl was, though she wouldn't be happy about it, she would support him. She would move by his side, in unison as she always had. Yeah, she'd support him, but she'd kick his ass for it later.

"Nitara!" He burst through the door calling out her name. This was not the time for gentle awakenings.

"Jinn?" His wife jumped from her content slumber and watched him hurriedly pack essentials to take. "What's wrong? What happened?"

"We have to go, now. We have to get out of here." He paused to catch her eye before continuing to move.

"What is going on? What did you do?" She jumped to her feet, moving to dress herself and help him pack. "Did you go to the village?" She knew her husband well.

"I'm sorry, I should have listened to you. We must go!"

Outside of their home, Jinn looked at the sky in the direction of the village. The dark cover was gone, but that absence made him more nervous than its presence ever had. He grabbed the reins of their horses, aiding Nitara in her climb. Atop his own steed, he gave a slight tap on its side and the horse took off running.

Hooves pounded the ground, as they raced forward, attempting to escape the monster Jinn had just faced. The prickly feeling at the back of his neck told him that they weren't doing a great job of it, yet still they forged on. Deep in the woods, away from main roads, he thought it safer travel for dodging a foe. Unfortunately, he was wrong. Explosions rang out, trees collapsed in unison, their bases fractured sending splinters in all direction. The wooden dagger launched right into his horse's side. His faithful steed bucked, knocking Jinn to the ground, its blood pouring onto his owner as he ran off into the distance and collapsed. Nitara abandoned her own horse to get to her husband's side.

"Jinn, are you okay?"

He lifted his head, attempting to upright himself, only to feel dizzy and collapse back down. For the second time that night his skull had taken a beating, but this time the recovery was not so quick. His hand lifted to the back of his head, revealing blood when he touched the point of pain.

"Oh, no, Jinn," Nitara cried. "We have to get you out of here." With all her effort, she attempted to lift the man from the ground, tripping on the dress she wore and fell atop him.

"Nitara, you have to get out of here," he whispered his plea. "Get on your horse and go. Get to safety."

"I will not leave you, not like this." There was nothing she could use to help her get him off the ground. Her magic was not as strong as his. Once they left the coven, she stopped practicing. Jinn's gift was natural, he was born with it. Hers was something she had to work for. In that moment, she couldn't call the air to her, the elements ignored her plea.

"You must, before it is too late."

"I'd say your window for escape has passed," the deep sickening voice called out. Across the fallen trees, Nitara lifted her eyes from her husband in time to witness the dark form appear. A tall figure cloaked in shadows.

"Who are you? What do you want?" she called out. "Please, leave us alone!"

"My name is of no concern to you. I came here for the man; I will leave with him." The dark figure began to move, headed for the couple.

"You will do no such thing!" Nitara stood, placing herself between the shadowed figure and her injured husband.

"Oh, and what is it that you think you will do to stop me?" The man laughed and the tone of dark humor echoed softly around them. He continued forward, slowly emerging from the shadows.

"I'm warning you, stay back!" Nitara called out.

"Oh, really?" The shadowed man rushed forward, expecting to knock the woman over, but instead slammed head first into an invisible wall. Nitara, as shocked as he was at the power she displayed, managed to conjure a force strong enough to provide protection from their stalker. "Oh my, isn't this a wonderful development!" The man waited just five feet from her. "You're just as strong as he is, aren't you?"

"Leave us alone!" she screamed.

"You see, I'm afraid I simply cannot do that, dear." He looked up to the sky and Nitara followed his gaze. The sky turned dark, the bright moon above her erased in the process. The liquid matter then dropped from the sky in a storm that beat on her shield. She could still see him, smiling. He knew she would never be able to keep up the protection long enough. Though she tried, the force was too powerful to withstand. Nitara fell to the ground and was washed over with the dark substance that hardened as quickly as it touched her. Both she and Jinn were trapped, locked inside a stone tougher than any that was natural to the world.

She couldn't avoid the sight of the nameless man who chanted a spell above her. His words were foreign, but the tone was ominous, dripping with darkness. Behind him the shadows lifted from the ground and rejoiced as he marked their souls with his magic. She cried as she felt herself changing; the fibers of her being were mutating into something different, something more.

It felt as though he would never stop, he would continue his spell for an eternity, and she would be forced to listen. However, he did stop and with his last words, Ignis Immortalem, the foreign stone crumbled, returned to its liquid state, and drew away from her. There wasn't a trace of it left, even her tattered dress was left unmarked. Her impulse was to crawl to her husband, to be sure he was safe.

"I'm sorry, Nitara," he whispered, still unable to move from the spot on the ground where he fell. His head continued to bleed from the wound.

"It's okay," she lied, and planted her lips against his. "We're okay."

"Oh, how touching." The man stood over them. "I'm afraid this affection must end now." From his cloak he pulled out two bottles. "Good thing I always carry a spare." He popped the cap of one and held it out to Nitara. "Come along now, dear."

Though she held on to her husband, clinging to him, the vacuum forced her into the vessel that would become her unwanted home. With tears in her eyes she gave him one last kiss before she lost hold of him.

"Well, it looks as if it's your turn." He put the bottle containing Nitara away and aimed the other at Jinn. "Let's not make a fight of this, huh? You need to rest; I have big plans for you!"

CHAPTER
NINETEEN

Praia watched in horror as Jinn relived the tragedy of his past. His body jerked and seized over and over. He screamed out his wife's name again and again as beads of sweat formed on his body, soaking the shirt he wore and gluing his hair to his forehead—he shook all over as once again he experienced the change that occurred when Daegal stripped away all that made him human. His magic was forced to transform into something dark. Praia watched it all in horror, fighting the urge to wake him from his state, but knowing she could not. Whatever he was experiencing, as hard as it was to witness, was a necessary piece of his journey. Jinn would kill her if she interrupted him.

Before she could do something stupid, the shaking stopped.

His body calmed, the strain melted from his features, leaving his face tranquil, and he breathed a sigh of relief before returning to a stoic state.

༄ᎫᎩ

Jinn's mind rushed forward as he was released from the past. No longer was he trapped inside the vessel, experiencing the suffocating feeling of his first possession. He breathed deeply, shaking off the cerebral heaviness of the experience, and took in his new surroundings. The space was a familiar one he'd only seen before in a vision given to him by Sybella. Dark, dingy surroundings with very little light to offer view of the contents of the space. Cages filled with djinn both familiar and not, only this time, when he noticed the chanting of nearby witches, he felt the pressure of their words on his body. Looking down at his hands, he noticed the bars in his clutch, but the hands were not his own. Small, dainty, and with a scar he recognized from a burn during a camp fire.

Nitara. He thought her name, realizing the spell hadn't worked quite the way he'd hoped it to.

Jinn? Her voice returned to him. *Jinn, is that you?*

Nitara, I am here. He felt the skip of her heart and it matched his own.

Where? I don't see you. Are you here? She whipped her head around, studying the area and giving him better sight of the space.

In your mind, Nitty. I am here. He called her by her pet name and felt the momentary warmth followed by an overwhelming feeling of worry.

I'm going crazy, aren't I? Their magic is starting to work on me like it did the others.

No, you're not going crazy. I'm coming to find you, I promise. I will get you out of here.

Where are you? She had hope ... not much of it, but it was there. His words, his presence, returned a bit of optimism back to her mind. Someone was looking for her, someone was trying to set her free.

I'm safe, with the fairies. I'm looking for you. He paused. *Nitty, do you know where you are?*

She looked out the small window that gave view of the sky. *Yes, I think so. It's hard to tell, we were moved around a lot.*

Where do you think? Your best guess is all I need.

Cascades. That is what I overheard them talking before the last move. The witch was to put us all to sleep, but I managed to fight it long enough to hear. I'm not sure if that is where we are but that's our final destination for sure.

Are you sure?

Yes. Actually, we may already be here. I often hear the cries of dragons. I believe it's mating season for them. Her mind began to wander and lose focus. He could feel it, she was weakening—the spell was starting to work on her just as she feared.

Good. I'm coming for you.

Jinn. She snapped back into focus, with urgency in her mind and heart. Nitara was afraid.

Yes, Nitty?

Hurry. What he is planning …

What is it?

He wants to take over. There is an eclipse coming. He has the stones. If he can keep the eclipse in place long enough, he can take down both fae and fairies. He has ordered us to make it so, she told him, revealing the plan that Daegal had shared with the djinn. The guy always had a big mouth, he felt the need to brag on his genius designs. He also made them swear to never speak a word of it to anyone should they get free. Technically, she hadn't broken her promise since he said nothing about thinking it inside her cell.

You're still tied to your vessel? How else would Daegal be able to force her to do anything she didn't want?

No, I was wished free, but his magic made us, we must obey. The witches keep us here, locked down until he is ready to use us. If we get far enough away, it fades. He keeps us close by to be sure we won't overpower his wishes or the coven that keeps us locked here with their spells. That is why we move so much.

Dammit.

Jinn, please be careful. She knew how reckless he could be, how he abandoned safety and common sense when he was on one of his save the world kicks. It wasn't the first time, and it wouldn't be the last time. That was who he was.

I will. I love you, Nitara.

I love you, too.

Her voice faded from his mind, and his eyes were his own again. The tough yet somber fae sat across from him, and her face dripped with worry. He wiped the tears from his eye before addressing the girl who looked like she was barely holding herself from attacking him with hugs. There was no experience as intense as reliving an event from the past. He'd done it before, but nothing as impactful as that day. He pushed through the emotions, the sorrow, and the hatred that he felt. "What?" He stared at her. "Why are you looking at me like that?"

"You … I, thought you were dying." She sighed, relieved to hear the normality in his voice.

"I told you it would be intense." He smiled at her as she stood from the floor, shaking her arms and legs to rid them of jitters. "What happened?"

"Just as you said. For a while you were so still, like someone had carved a replica of you in stone. I was ready to sit here counting the number of grey hairs that are creeping into your beard, but then you began to tremble like you were cold but sweat formed at your brow as if you were burning up. Then there was the screaming, mixed in with gut-wrenching yells. You called out Nitara's name a lot. It was as if you were suffering, like you were being tortured."

"That's not far off from what was happening." He stood from the floor without aide though he felt exhausted, stretched his limbs, and wiped the remaining sweat from his forehead. His hair had come loose from the holder which was clinging to just a handful of his locks, the rest was hanging around his face. As he stretched, he moved the strands back to their intended place bound by the band. "I'm sorry you had to witness that but thank you for being here."

"Well, did it work? Did you find him?" Praia eyed him eagerly, wanting to know every detail about his experience.

"In a way." The corners of his lips lifted just slightly. "I know where they are."

"Really? Where?" She lifted a brow, wondering what he meant by, 'in a way.'

"They're in the Cascades." He began to exit the chamber. They needed to let the others know, and he needed to prepare for a trip.

"Shit." She followed behind him, gathering the blankets and incense he'd lit. Before she could grab all of the items, he snapped his fingers and they vanished.

"Yeah," he laughed dryly, "my sentiments exactly."

"You mean to tell me he has dragons on his side?" If that were true, they would have a much bigger problem on their hands.

Dragons brought an entirely new element to the fight.

"I can't say what he has, but that is where they are, and there are other witches working with him." He stopped at the door. "Daegal's a talented man. He would have no trouble convincing dragons to join him. If they have, it's because he has made a deal with them, promised them a piece of the pie when all this is done."

"You know this for sure? About the witches, are there more than the ones you saw before?"

"Yes, the spell didn't work exactly as I imagined and instead of finding Daegal, I was with Nitara. In her mind, her eyes were my own. We spoke." He smiled, remembering the sound of her voice. Though she was trapped, she was still strong, the only of the djinn that remained standing, not crumpled on the floor. "There were three witches in the chamber with Nitara and the others. The spell is one to bind them, but it isn't working, not completely. Nitara has been able to withstand them, not entirely, but enough that she was able to overhear where they'd taken them. There has to be more. They chant continuously, which means they are taking shifts. If they stop, the djinn will be able to get free and Daegal will not be pleased."

"Whoa." Praia smiled, ignoring the vital information he'd just given her and thinking only of Jinn and the subtle glow of hope he had. "You spoke to her? Is she okay? How do you feel?" She rattled off the questions giddily.

"Yes, I saw her. She is okay, I think. She is strong." He laughed at the expression on Praia's face. "I must admit, I feel better knowing she doesn't hate me. She doesn't blame me."

"Good!" Praia could no longer contain herself—she leapt forward and hugged the man who nearly doubled her in size. "I'm so happy for you, Jinn. We will get her. We will save her, and the two of you will live happily ever after." She paused. "I'll still get steaks though, right?"

"Yeah, let's hope so." He returned her embrace before she released her hold and hopped back to the floor, her mind was once again focused on plotting out their next move.

"Wait, you said that the witches are using a spell to bind them. Why?" The analytical side of her brain kicked back into gear as they continued out into the hall.

"They were all wished free, none of them are tied to their vessels anymore. Their freedom makes their magic that much more powerful, like mine. He can force them to do as he wishes because his magic created them, so they are bonded to him. However, he needs to make sure they do not get away, hence the cages. It seems the requests he make only take hold for a short period of time."

"Meaning to keep them there he would have to continuously ask them to stay." The cogs in her brain turned as she pieced it together

"Correct."

"So, this all-powerful warlock who created you, and however many other djinns, is held up in the land of dragons, who hate us by the way, and also has the help of witches," she recapped the news he'd provided.

"That about sums it up," he confirmed as they reached the door to Briar's temporary office. Eventually she would have to move into the chambers she avoided.

"What is his plan?" They waited as the guard went inside to announce their arrival and get permission for them to enter.

"I'm not sure of that exactly, but I do know that by going near him, I will be giving him the advantage." Jinn held back the news of the eclipse. He needed to figure out a solution before he brought the issue at hand to them.

"What is it?" Praia touched his arm. "You're keeping something from me."

"The same magic that made them, made me. I'm bound to him just as they are." There it was, the risk that he would be taking. Daegal could very well claim him just as he had the others.

"Yet, you're still ready to go there and face him?"

"I have to. It's Nitara, I have to save her."

CHAPTER
TWENTY

"I know what he wants!" Praia barged into the meeting room that Briar had claimed as her space.

"What?" Briar stood, holding her hand out to the guards who had blocked Praia's path. They stood down and the fae girl continued forward. Praia wasn't one for formalities. She'd grown up very close to the king in her home, and her intrusions were never seen as a problem.

"Sorry, I still forget your new status here." She bowed slightly, a show of respect which felt weird to them both.

"It's okay. To be honest, I still forget myself." She pointed to the seat next to her, inviting the girl to join her. "What have you found?"

"Daegal, I figured it out." Jinn hadn't told them what Nitara told him about the warlock's plans, but Praia was persistent. She'd taken to the archives both in her own home and in Vilar. The heavy books thudded, the boom echoed through the space, as they hit the table in front of the queen.

"Okay, what's your theory?" Briar hadn't even looked at the books, wanting to hear what Praia had to say. It wasn't as if she could decipher the answer faster than the girl could speak.

"Look at this." She pulled the books apart, revealing the images on the front. The black book held the symbol of the sun, the white book, the symbol of the moon. "He took both of our peoples' stones, the Solaris and the Lunaire. Stones representing both the sources of our power, the sun, and the moon. Right?"

"Yes, so?"

"So, think about it! What if he could use them to somehow stop us from connecting with those sources." She paused, allowing Briar to catch up with her. When the dark eyes widened, Praia continued. " Exactly! It would cripple our forces. It would give him the upper hand. Without our powers, we're no better than the humans!"

"Okay, say this is his plan. How?" Briar sat at the table, now enthralled in the story she was being told. "How could he make this happen?"

"The eclipse."

"Eclipse?"

Praia opened both books to marked pages. Both read the same

text. The Darkest Hour. Praia read it aloud. "During the darkest hour, when the eclipse is above, the power of the moon is no more." She looked at Briar who hadn't caught on just yet. "Don't you get it? During the eclipse, fae cannot connect to the power of the moon, the sun's energy blocks it." She turned the Solaris book to Briar. "It says the exact same thing in your book. When the eclipse is here, the moon blocks the power of the sun."

"He is going to attack during the eclipse and disconnect us from our power." Briar's eyes lifted from the book to Praia who held the same expression of fear. "We will be powerless against him if he should succeed in this."

"Exactly, and it gets worse. We have three days to find him." She placed the lunar calendar which had been rolled up in her back pocket on the table. It showed the progression of the moon and sun, marking each time there would be an eclipse. "The next one is in just a few days. This is only a theory, but our stones are connected to the sun and moon. I think Daegal knows about the bond that is there. I believe somehow, he plans to use the stones and harness the power of those djinns he has captured. If he can do that, he can make the eclipse last."

"Long enough to take us all down." Briar fell back into her seat. "Fuck."

"Exactly." Praia finally sat down. With her news delivered, her mind could rest long enough to realize how tired she was. She hadn't slept since Jinn left them.

"We have to get to him before that happens." Briar poured them both a glass of wine. "You did really good here." She passed the glass to Praia who happily accepted it.

"How? We have an army behind us here, but there, in Dragon territory?" She sipped the sweet dark liquid and sighed. "I don't know about the fairy connections, but we fae have no friends there."

"We're going to have to call in a favor." Briar stood from the table and exited the room.

Gathering the books and calendar, Praia convinced her tired body to move and followed behind her. "Favor, from who?"

Briar looked back over her shoulder with worried eyes. "An old friend."

❦

"Wow." Praia bowed to the queen as she entered the chamber room. It was the first time since becoming queen that Briar had dressed the part. She'd traded her standard black wardrobe for a gown that draped to the floor in various hues of orange and red that were compliments to the dark tones of her skin. Her hair was pulled up in a tight bun and decorated with flowers and jewels. From her shoulders hung a sheer cape only slightly darker than the dress beneath it. Stitched in gold on the back was the Solaris stone.

"I must look the part, right?' Briar smiled despite how awkward she felt in her new attire.

"Oh, you do. You're beautiful." Praia sighed, eyes glowing with admiration for the woman who stood in front of her.

"Thank you, Praia." She smiled. "And thank you for agreeing to be here with me today. I know it is not easy considering the dragons do not show favor to our kind."

"We're in this together." The short fae smiled. When Jinn left, she promised to stay and help Briar with whatever she needed. Praia wasn't one to break a promise.

The doors opened and Mysti approached. "My queen, your guest has arrived."

"See him in, please." Briar gave the order and took a deep breath, one that helped to calm her nerves.

"Briar! How nice to be summoned, and by the queen no less!" the bold voice of an old acquaintance rang out, echoing slightly against the high ceilings. The tall, slender man walked in draped in a black cloak which covered a suit tailored to perfection. She hadn't seen Jax, the Prince of the Dragons, in decades. Behind him stood a stoic dragon who scoped the room, a security check to be sure the prince was not in danger. Outside in the hall, with the rest of the fairy guard, were three other dragons, and outside the building were twenty more. There was no trust, obviously.

"Jax, thank you for coming," Briar spoke with a wide grin.

She was never one to fake a smile, but apparently it came with the territory. She couldn't very well greet the man with a grimace and then ask him for a favor.

"Hey, you and I go way back, of course." He smiled and handed his escort the cloak. "Tell me, how can I be of service to you? I assume you called me here for more than to just show off your pretty new crown." His eyes took her in, since he'd never seen her dolled up in such a way. "I like the makeover by the way."

"You're right, I do have more important reasons for your being here, none of which include the updates to my attire." She held back her own comments about the bright red he'd dyed his hair. The dragon must have been going through some sort of personal crisis to do something like that. "Our people are being threatened, and I need your assistance."

"Ah, so the rumors are true. Your queen suddenly gone, though I know you tried to hide the details. But you know how tales tend to travel." He paced the floor, knowing he had the upper hand. She needed something from him, which meant he could make a deal in his favor. "I'm guessing this is connected to the fae misfortunes as well, considering your current companion." He looked over his shoulder at Praia who rolled her eyes.

"Yes, that is true."

"So, fill me in."

"We have done our research. We know who poses a threat to our people, and we're fairly sure what his plan is. We just need to find a way to stop him before he gets there." He continued to pace the floor, but she had his attention, so she said, "His name is Daegal, a warlock with great power. We have sources that tell us he is in the Cascades."

"Sources lie," Jax snapped back. "Are you accusing us of something?"

"Jax—" she began.

"Look, I know my land, and I know my people, there is no Daegal in Cascades." His jaw tightened, and for a moment so quick she barely caught it, his eyes flashed red.

"No, that is not what I'm doing. I would not have invited you here simply to accuse you of any wrong doing." He settled back into his placid pacing. "Like I said, he is very powerful. Perhaps he used that power to find a way inside, without you knowing about it." Briar considered the avenues the warlock would be willing to take, and she was unable to rule out anything. Including bribing a dragon, even if Jax thought it improbable. "Can you be sure that no dragon would have aided him?"

"There is no one." He spoke quickly and turned away from her.

"You still have that tell; you know. It gives you away every time." She eased in closer. Jax never played any games with Briar because she could always tell when he was bluffing. "You suspect something, or someone. Who is it?"

"I don't know what you're talking about." Jax casually increased the distance between them, pretending to be admiring the details in the decoration of the space.

"Jax, come on, let's drop the games, this is serious." She could only coax him for so long. The queenly way was still new to her; the old Briar pushed to the surface.

"Look, Bri, I really wish I could help you, but I can't." He was near the exit, ready to walk away from the entire mess. The dragons had no stake in the fairy problems, and he wouldn't be volunteering their sources on a hunch. There had to be more in it for him if he was going to convince his father to go along with what she wanted.

"I'll tell you where she is." She'd hoped not to have to use her trump card, she'd hoped that he would be willing to help without a bribe. She knew it would never happen that way, but she still had hope. Very minute hope, but hope, nonetheless.

"Excuse me?" His leisurely progression toward the exit ended. He wanted her to make it worth his time, and she'd done just that.

"I know you have been looking for her, all these years, wondering where she is. I know where she is." It always came down to a girl, Briar knew that. Throughout the years she'd watch so many men risk everything for the love of a woman. Jinn was doing the same, and Jax was no different.

"That's a game you don't want to play, Briar." The flesh at his neck tensed and momentarily scaled over, but he was able to push the transition back. A shift in the middle of a fairy city, inside of the queen's chamber, would be an act of war no matter what their relationship was in the past.

"I'm not playing any games with you, Jax. Inda is alive and well. She will likely kill me for telling you, but at this point, I'm fresh out of options. I need your help, and if you want to see her again, well, you need mine." Jax had to have a stake in the game. He was like all the other dragons—stubborn, hardheaded, and believed he was above the troubles of the world. Daegal would come for them next, without a doubt, but Jax wasn't concerned with possible yet uncertain futures.

"You have some guts, bringing me here to blackmail me." He walked back over to her, heat raising from his skin. "If you were any other person, this would go a very different way."

"You knew what this was when you came, why else would I call you here?" Briar stood her ground, her own temper rising. She wished she'd opted for combat gear instead of the formal wear. If Jax wanted a fight, she would give him one. "You knew I needed help and you came ready for a bargain, to make a deal. Well, here is your offer. You help me get this bastard, and you get your girl back … that is if she will take you back." Briar shrugged. "All I can do is get you in the same room."

Jax thought about the offer. He made a show of it by rubbing his chin and resuming his pacing, but Briar knew she had him where she wanted him. "I can grant you and your people safe passage, just let me know when you plan to come." He would have to convince his father, but with recent changes, Jax was being given more responsibilities and more authority. There wouldn't be much resistance. "I will return to the Cascades and do some digging. If I come across anything, I'll let you know."

"Thank you." She nodded in appreciation of his agreement to her terms and indicated for the aid to retrieve his coat.

"What of my information?" He took the coat from the small fairy and turned a hard gaze on Briar.

"I'm no fool, Jax. Keep up your end, and I will keep mine."

"You know, the queen thing fits you." He smiled, knowing the statement was much more of a dig than he let on. Briar never wanted to be queen. She'd told him plenty times that it was not something she desired to ever have to deal with. Jax left the room wearing a wide grin and tossing his cloak to hang over his shoulder from two fingers.

"Do you trust him?" Praia questioned when the doors closed, sealing the two inside the room alone again.

"Yeah, we were friends at one point, before the wars turned our people into enemies. I swear," Briar returned to the seat she'd avoided for so long, and slouched into it, "this was all supposed to be so much better than what we had before. Look at us, we're horrible! Wars and killing, and people kept in cages. There are children out there living like animals, we are worse than the humans. We did all this claiming to have a better way, to be able to fix this world, and here it is worse than it ever was in the hands of the humans. We are a plague, all of us. Sometimes I really wish we had never been revealed. I wish that we had kept on living as we were. At least then, things made sense. Then, I could look out on the world and hope to be able to make a real change. Now? Now all I see is more pain, more hurt, more fear than I ever saw before."

"You can do something about it, you already are," Praia stated softly. She realized Briar was in a bad way. With everything moving so quickly, the woman never had a chance to stop and mourn. She was second in command to the queen, they were best friends, and she was gone. To top that off, Briar was forced to be reminded of her every second of every day. Each meeting, briefing, and conference call she'd had to attend, called Alesea to mind.

"Yeah, okay." Briar sighed and dropped her head back to look up through the glass ceiling to the sun above.

"You're the queen now, and maybe you didn't want that, but you are." Praia moved to the base of the steps that led to the throne. "That means you have the power to make change. In a way, you're already doing that. You've helped Mike and his people, which is a way toward peace between the fairies and the slithers. You've just gotten Jax to help, which yeah, okay, was kind of blackmail, but it also means you have a way to connect with his people. And then there is me, fae, wandering the halls of your home freely and not one fairy here has ever made me feel like I'm not welcome to be here. That is because they are loyal to you. They trust your decision, your gut instinct about me and every other choice you've made. They will follow you toward the peace that you are hoping to achieve." She sighed, hoping her words were getting through. "Many people dream to be able to change the world. They hope that in some small way, they can make an impact. You actually have the means to do it. You have a platform, a voice, use it the way you would have wanted Alesea, or any other queen before her to use it."

"You're right. I have to do more; I have to make a change." Briar sat up in the throne. "Thank you, Praia."

"Any time." The fae smiled, happy that they were becoming friends.

"What was that about?" Mysti entered the room, having escorted Jax and his men away from Vilar. Once out of the city, they took flight, back to the Cascades.

"That was about Briar getting us the help we need to get into the Cascades. We have less than two days left before the eclipse," Praia answered without thinking. She caught her mistake and apologized. Eventually she would get used to Briar's status as queen.

"I need you to get word to Mike and his people," the queen instructed her second. "We need the strongest, we're taking the fight to him." Briar stood. "Praia get the fae together, we need all the help we can get. We'll have to use magic to transport us, there is no time for any other way."

CHAPTER
TWENTY
ONE

J inn left Vilar after speaking with Briar about what he'd learned
from Nitara. Still keeping the secret of Degal's plan. If they
hadn't figured it out by his return, he would tell them then.
Realizing where they would be headed and just what they were
up against, Jinn knew they would need a lot more help. Though his
friends were few and far in between, there were still a few people in
his debt. He left it that way, for a time such as this.

Since the war, Earth had taken a turn for the better. If there
was anything to be said for the transition of power, it was the
rejuvenation of the earth. Places that had been all but wiped clean
of their resources flourished again. The ozone was being repaired,

in large amounts due to the fae and fairy magic. Which meant the world was able to cool down again with the discontinuation of human manufacturing. The polar ice caps were restored by the ice dragons who used the area for their mating season. Even if the inhabitants of Earth hadn't quite figured their shit out, the planet itself was prospering.

Jinn stood on the snow-covered lands of Antarctica. He hadn't been to the area in years and it took his breath away to see just how much the place had changed. It was majestic and terrifying all at the same time. Even with his power, the cold threatened him. If exposed too long to the elements, he would suffer just as anyone else. He pulled the parka he'd conjured around himself tighter.

The entrance to the hideout was just up ahead. It was kept in the frozen lands, because much like the scorched lands, no one wanted to live there. Where no one wanted to go, a person looking to lay low would thrive. Of course he would need the help of an outlaw … who better to take down a warlock gone dark?

He lifted his hand to the tall wall that appeared as a thick slab of ice, meant to deceive any unwanted visitors. The familiar signature of an old acquaintance. Blue light emanated from his hand, a key for a door only those like him could unlock, and the hidden passage opened to him, revealing a long hall and the sound of opera music. Jinn stepped inside and the exit sealed behind him, causing the music to echo around him.

Cautiously he moved forward, walking down the hall to the source of the sound. The light just ahead—produced by carefully placed candles—glowed, giving some light to the hall; not a lot, but enough so that he wouldn't trip or need to conjure any of his own. He didn't want to alert the resident of his arrival just yet. Better to scope the situation out, and make sure his old pal hadn't gone insane after being in solitude for so long. If he determined the guy would be of no use, he could leave without incident. As he reached the end of the hall, he could see that his friend was in good mind and spirits. Jinn stood in the doorway, looking at the fool who danced in front of him with a person he knew didn't really exist.

"Well, I see you've got yourself a new girlfriend." Jinn laughed and leaned his shoulder against the frame of the door.

The oversized man stumbled backwards, startled by his voice. "Shit, you nearly gave me a heart attack!" He waved his hand, and his curvy blonde dance partner faded into nothing, leaving trails of orange smoke behind. "Hell, you know I was always one for a good dance."

"You're still the only person I know to dance to opera." Jinn shook his head. "How the hell have you been, Bruto?"

"As good as a djinn in hiding can be. Did you come here to tell me all my enemies have died, and I can go free?" Bruto, an oversized djinn with red hair and skin so pale he could be mistaken for a vampire, flashed a bright smile hopeful for good news.

"No, I'm not here with news of the apocalypse." Jinn chuckled and looked around the place. It had long since been transformed from the cavern of ice he'd left Bruto with. Of course, the djinn had all the magic in the world and could make the place into whatever he pleased. For Bruto, that meant making the space bigger. Tall ceilings with chandeliers all powered by candlelight, which seemed a bit risky considering the structure, but the flames weren't real, they were conjured elements meant for show. Large canvases of classical art hung on display, covering nearly every wall. The walls themselves were solid, not ice, painted brown with false windows that gave display to images of the hills of Ireland. The floor was a beautiful hardwood that tied the space together. At the back of the room he could see two double doors. Bruto had done some expansion on the place.

"Well, come on in, and tell me what brings you to the frozen tundra." The djinn was welcoming, happy for a real person to converse with.

Jinn walked further into the room, noting all of the possessions the man had conjured for himself. He was living the good life, a free djinn, only not. Bruto had a lot of enemies, and though he was strong, he was no match for the entire collective of the witches of the Ashen. Convincing him to take part in the expedition was going to be a tough gig. Jinn had the upper hand, though. He'd saved Bruto's life on more than one occasion, the last time being the most dire situation the man had ever been in.

Bruto pulled out a seat at the large table that sat to the left side of the room and indicated that Jinn should take the one across from him. As Jinn sat, two cups of coffee appeared. With the steam rising from the mug, he could smell that there was much more than coffee.

"A little early for whiskey, don't you think?" He eyed the beverage.

"Not when its Molly's Irish Cream!" Bruto winked and smiled at Jinn knowing he'd hit a weak spot.

"How the hell did you get some of that?" Jinn leaned in and smelled it. "This seems fresh, not conjured."

"Let's just say I had an in." Bruto laughed a deep chuckle that resonated around them.

"Yeah, I don't even want to know." Jinn lifted the mug to his lips, taking a sip of the beverage, and allowed the flavor to wash over him. Mentally he was transported back to his time in Ireland where he'd run into Bruto. At the time, the djinn was on the run, just after he'd pissed off a strong witch who would come to be one of the High Council for the Collective. Jinn helped him escape her, and when the Collective was formed, he helped to hide the djinn from the covens.

"So, you were going to tell me why you're here." Jinn savored his drink, but he knew Bruto understood that he hadn't showed up for a cordial visit.

"Yes." He took another sip before placing the beverage back on the table. "I'm here to cash in on a favor."

"As you mentioned. What is it that you need?"

"I need you to help me fight a powerful warlock of the Collective and stop him from wiping out both the fae and the fairies." His words were like the ice outside the cavern, they brought a frost to the room that stilled the phony flames that danced and threw their light against the walls.

The soft operatic music that had been playing in the background stopped and Bruto sat straight up in his chair and abandoned the relaxed position he previously had. "You need me to do what? Are you out of your mind?"

"No, I'm completely sane." He took another sip of his drink. "Right now I really wish that I could claim that I was a few marbles shy."

"Why would I risk everything, risk getting caught out there to help a bunch of Tinker Bell wannabes who never lifted a finger to help me?" Bruto leaned forward, ready for the answer. Jinn knew it had better be a damned good one if he wanted to convince him to help.

"Because, they aren't the ones asking for your help. I am, and you owe me."

"Yeah, man, but damn." He stood up, pacing in front of Jinn. He wanted to get out of his lonely sentence to the icebox, but not to go to war with the same people he went into hiding to avoid!

"He has Nitara." It was time to drop the bomb—no amount of convincing would work otherwise. Bruto was a man of passion, he needed to have a stake in the game, something he cared about.

"What?" The large man paused his movement, turning his gaze to Jinn who remained in his seat.

"Yeah, he has Nitara, and a few others as well." Jinn never liked how much Bruto liked his wife, but in this case, it worked for the cause.

"I thought she died." He perked up, happy to hear that the woman he once mourned was alive and well.

"That seems to be what he wanted us to think." Jinn couldn't be sure that Daegal was the one who falsified reports of her death, but it made sense. If everyone thought she was dead, no one would come looking for her. Including Jinn.

"Shit, man."

Jinn knew he had him. If there was even a chance that he would deny lending a hand, it went out the window when Nitara came into the picture. Bruto looked at her like a sister. The two became very close when Jinn was unable to be with her, and when Bruto lost his own wife, a mortal who wished him free, it was Nitara who helped him through it. For a while, it was a bond that Jinn hated, but he'd learn to move on from it considering he was never around them when they knew one another. Their time together was one he'd never gotten to witness, and he was glad for it. Bruto may have been one very dead djinn if Nitara had fawned over the man in front of her husband.

"So, I can count on your help?" Taking the last sip of his coffee and wishing there was more to continue the warm buzz that had spread over him, Jinn stood from his seat.

"Yeah, you got it." Bruto paused. "Anything for Nitara. I mean, for you, too, but especially for her." His solitary laughter was cut by Jinn's following remark.

"Great, because we need to go get Rosie." If he hadn't been afraid the man would change his mind, Jinn would have laughed at the mixed expression on Bruto's face. It was a look of disgust, fear, and somehow, enthusiasm.

"Fuck, Jinn! Was it your plan to destroy my entire night?"

"We need the old team, man." He shrugged. "No way I can do what I need to do without everyone on board."

"Right, the old team, plus a hag of a woman who will try to bite my head off the moment she sees me." Bruto shook the red hair atop his head and a thick parka appeared around him. "Let's go get the old woman, shall we?"

༎ J ༎

It wasn't a long journey to find Rosie, and Jinn found humor in the location she chose to claim her home. Of course, she would tell them that it was merely a coincidence her residence just happened to be in close proximity to the man she swore to the heavens above she couldn't stand to be around for more than a few moments. On a small island not too far off the coast of Argentina was about as close as she could get without being in the frozen Antarctic where Bruto dwelled.

Once known as South Georgia, she'd somehow managed to

make the place all her own, casting a cloak that made it so only a djinn could locate it. To anyone else it would be as if it vanished off the map. As there weren't many of them left, there was no concern of anyone ruining her peace. Jinn assumed she made it that way because she knew one day, they would come looking for her. Or, she hoped that Bruto would escape his solitary and stumble across her new home. He'd be able to hide out there, free of worry about the Collective coming for him.

Rosie had been very thorough in her takeover of the land; all evidence of its former human inhabits had been wiped out. Not that there had been much to eliminate. Even at its peak, the place only housed about fifty people. Instead of campsites and survey points, there were penguins everywhere.

"This is freaky, man," Bruto commented as he stepped around the waddling birds. "Why are there so many here?"

"She always had a thing for them, especially the babies. What did she used to say?" Jinn tried to recall her affectionate squawking, but Bruto was right on the money.

"Oh!" Bruto raised his voice about ten octaves, mimicking the squeal of their friend. "They're just so fluffy and cuddly and I just wanna smoosh them!" He picked up a baby bird, rubbing his face into its fir, and quickly put it down after an adult penguin started attacking his leg, jabbing its beak into his shin. "Damn, ouch!"

"And that is exactly what you get for making fun of me!" Rosie laughed as she floated over to them above her penguin babies. She, unlike the others, sported the garb of a genie drawn in a children's book. Where Jinn and Bruto wore jeans, T-shirts, and boots, Rosie wore sheer purple harem pants with a matching top that left her belly button on display as if it wasn't thirty degrees outside. She cared nothing about hiding her extra curves, proudly flaunting the pudge at her sides and the stretch marks that were the result of her packing on a few extra pounds. Her hair was pulled up into a high ponytail that fell around her face in full locks of candy red with white streaks. It looked like she had candy canes hanging from her head. "Have some manners, boys. Feet off the ground!"

Obeying her request, both Jinn and Bruto lifted from the ground. They floated above the penguins, one of whom was still eyeballing Bruto. He would be no fan favorite there.

"Now, why are you here." She looked to Bruto with eyes that seemed too large for her face. "Why are you not in hiding?"

"Jinn needed my help, so here I am. Nothing more to it." He smirked. "Don't act like you aren't thrilled to see me."

She scowled at him and then replied, "Must be pretty damn major to have convinced you to come out and face the Ashen."

"It is. That's why we're here asking for your help as well," Jinn spoke up.

"Hmm, well it seems we have a lot to discuss, boys. Follow me." She turned from them but paused and threw a pointed glance over her shoulder. "Oh, and, Bruto, do try to keep your hands off the penguins."

Rosie had built her home, a not so subtle castle done in shades of pink and purple, at the highest peak of the island on top of Mount Paget. She'd carved out the top, crafting a lush home where a chosen few penguins joined her after she'd done a bit of magic to condition them for life at that altitude.

"Pepper, I'm home!" she called out, and a short emperor penguin with a damaged wing waddled up to her. Pepper nuzzled against her leg, before jerking his head at the unexpected guests. "Oh, they are my friends, honey. Don't worry." She patted his head and strolled on. "Come on in, fellas!"

Rosie lived much like Bruto; in extravagance. Her home was a plush stereotype, the typical thought of what the inside of a genie's bottle would look like. She'd actually taken a few designer tips from the television show. She had no problem with playing into the portrayal of her character. She was one of the few who didn't gag at the images plastered across the world of what a djinn really looked like. Sure, they all lived above a puff of smoke and were extravagant in everything they did. Jinn always felt it was tiring, the way the world thought he lived.

She led them into a sitting room. The walls were rounded and lined in plush cushions that were upholstered in variations of neon colors. Plopping down atop the mountain of fluff, she waited for her old friends to get comfortable.

"Rosie," Jinn began, as he desperately tried to situate himself without the feeling of sinking into the plush padding beneath his ass, "I'm here to ask something pretty drastic of you."

"Yes, so you alluded to earlier. What is it?" A floating tray of crackers, cheese, and fruits passed through the room, offering its contents to the guests. Jinn declined, but Bruto stuffed his face with grapes and cubes of sharp cheddar.

"In a nutshell, a powerful warlock of the Ashen has Nitara and I need your help to save her," Jinn spit it out, which was the best way to rip the Band-Aid clean off. Just as Bruto had, Rosie processed his announcement with an expression of shock on her face, but quickly put the pieces together.

"Nitara..." She paused, pondering the name she hadn't heard in ages. "So she isn't dead, and he has her trapped somehow."

"Yes," he replied, "and it's Daegal."

Recognizing the name, Bruto choked. He never thought to ask who the guy was. The name was one that brought back an instant replay of a collection of nightmares.

Rosie frowned at the chunks of cheese that hit her floor. Bruto was a slob who she'd have to get out of her home as soon as possible. He did it on purpose, always had, anything to get a dig in at her. She waved a finger and the mess vanished. "Do you have a plan to set her free?"

"Working on it," Jinn responded. "There aren't as many of us left as I hoped. I haven't been able to find Maverick or any of the others."

"So, it's just the three of us then?" She stood from her seat with ease, while Jinn struggled to climb out of his.

"Yes," he grunted as he finally made it free. "Just us three."

"Right, well. Okay!" She clapped her hands. "I guess I should get my things together."

"What?" Bruto nearly choked on his cheese. "That's it?"

"Yes. What more do you want? Hell, I figure if it got your scary ass out of hiding then it must be serious." She patted the head of Pepper who was nuzzling her leg. "Besides, we all know the two of you can't do anything right if I'm not by your side."

"Yeah, right," Bruto huffed.

"Just give me a few moments to prepare myself and we shall be on our way." She headed out of the room. "Oh, I must figure out a system for my babies while I'm away."

"Babies?" Bruto guffawed and once again choked on a piece of cheese.

"Man, chew your food!" Jinn laughed and headed out of the room to find a normal chair to sit in.

CHAPTER
TWENTY
TWO

The Cascades were a gorgeous land. The moment the war kicked off; dragons made quick work of claiming the old grounds of New Zealand for their own. It was the perfect place for them with high hills, mountains, and woodland flushed with plenty of trees. There was ample space for new dragons to roam and learn the proper ways of a dragon's life. It was a complete paradise for their kind. Once they took hold, there was no fighting them for it. Their guards were skilled, and worthy opponents for anyone who dared to approach. The territory was filled with dragons of all sorts, not just those who breathed fire, but those who breathed ice, those who could fly and those who couldn't, and a few who dwelled in the waters around their land. Even the Komodo dragon, not supernatural in any way, called the place home.

Briar couldn't help but think about Inda. The last time she'd visited the Cascades, she was with her phoenix friend and they turned heads the moment they touched down. Dragons and phoenixes didn't have what someone would call a great history together. Jax loved Inda, but not everyone like him shared that feeling. There were a few instances that broke the rules, their relationship was one. Briar hadn't been to the Cascades since Inda left.

Inda was the love of Jax's life. Briar knew the dragon before he met her, and he was changed entirely when the bird of fire flew into his life. The suave ladies' man quickly changed his tone when it came to Inda. Yeah, for a while he kept up his façade as the womanizer, but the look in his eyes whenever she spoke, when she entered the room, or even when she was laying into him, was undeniable. He was in love and it changed him to his very core. He begged her to stay with him, but she had been called home. When the wars began, every phoenix left earth, returning to their realm for protection. Inda was called like all the others. Despite her love for Jax, she obeyed the orders and left him. The result was an epic fight, because she refused to say no to her people, and he was not allowed to go with her.

Though she promised to return to him as soon as she could, they both knew what the risk was in her leaving. Time in her realm was different than that of earth. A few days there was a few weeks on earth. Depending on how long they forced her to stay, decades could pass before she would return. Considering Earth was at war, neither believed it would be a quick turnaround. Jax worried that even though she may very well be the same woman when she returned, he would not be the same man. Inda begged him to understand, but Jax was stubborn and hot headed. He wanted her to stay and defy her people even though he couldn't say he would do the same for her. When Inda returned to Earth, along with the others like her, she couldn't stand to face him. So, for the last six years, she'd been back, and Jax was completely unaware. She made Briar promise not to tell him. Considering she had no contact with the man, it was a promise she had every intention of keeping, but times demanded she do whatever necessary to protect her people. Inda would curse her out, but she would forgive her … at least Briar hoped she would.

Jax had come through on his promise to provide their group safe passage through the Cascades. The word had been put out to the masses, no one was to interfere. The problem with the broadcast was that it also meant that Daegal would know that they were coming. Odds were, whoever helped him, received word as well. So much for a surprise attack. It didn't really matter much. They had thirty-six hours left to find him and stop his plan from coming to fruition.

"Briar." Jax stepped back and looked at the large group she'd brought with her. The eclectic group was unexpected to say the least. There were several types of supernatural creatures that made up their ranks, from bear shifters to fae. "You have a very interesting group here," he stated with a wide smile, surprised that she had been able to get so many willing to aid her.

She ignored his jab. "Jax, thank you for helping us."

"No problem. I am a man of my word." He lowered his voice to whisper, "Let's hope your word is as valuable."

"You know that it is." She rolled her eyes at the insult. She was the queen—to give her word and go back on it would make not only her, but all her people look bad. She would never do such a thing.

"Great, so I have a few friends who will assist you in your travels. We have an inkling of where our unapproved visitor may be." Jax turned to the men who stood behind him, preparing to introduce them.

"You're not coming with us?" Briar asked, having hoped he would join them in their fight.

"No, I have other things to tend to." Jax made it clear that her fight was not his own.

"Right …"

"As I was saying, there is a traitor amongst us. His name is Cast. He's an ice dragon who was disgraced after an unsuccessful attempt to kill our king, an attempt that should have resulted in the discontinuation of his life." His jaw tightened as he recalled the incident that left his father injured and on the brink of death.

"He tried to kill your father?" Briar reached out but dropped her hand when his eyes flashed red. They weren't friends regardless of his decision to help them.

"Yes. Fortunately, my brother, Quinn, was there. I'm not sure what he hoped to accomplish. He would have had to kill my father and his fifteen children to even have a hope of taking the throne. Even then, there are a series of officials who would have the right to claim the title long before he ever would. A lot of people think he was just out of it, completely unhinged. I'd say that is likely the truth. Either way, he was banished. He should have been killed, but my father took pity on the dragon who had no one else in his life. He forced him to the dark island. A piece of land quite like the scorched lands. It was uninhabitable, but he has made it his own and it would seem he has made a deal with your little friend. A recent survey of the island shows that life has returned to it. It's covered in foliage now. I'm assuming he is looking for power, enough power to finish the job he started, and thinks he can trust this warlock to grant him that."

"I can tell you now that he's playing a fool's game," Jinn spoke. Daegal was never one to make deals in which he had to give up something. If he'd made a deal with this Cast, the ice dragon was really the one indebted to the warlock. He may not be aware, but he would never be free of the darkness that came with dealing with the devil.

"You think so?" Jax turned to the djinn. He knew exactly who he was. "I take it you have firsthand knowledge of the warlock."

"What do you think he promised those witches who are

helping him now? They are no more than slaves, doing a continuous spell to keep his prisoners there. The moment they are not needed, he will toss them aside. I've seen it before." Jinn looked to his two companions, djinns like himself. Created and discarded because Daegal sought to create something, or someone stronger.

"You have?" Jax dug deeper. The better he understood their enemy, the better chance he had at finding a way to defeat him.

"Yes. After he turned us, we were made to stay with him." Bruto stepped forward, placing a hand on Jinn's shoulder. "I can't erase the memories of the things he did, and the people he used, all in the name of gaining more power. This man is ruthless, your Cast will likely not survive this."

"I can't say I care if Cast survives." Jax laughed. If he had his way, the ice dragon would have been taken out a long time ago. "What happened? How did you get free?"

"Luck, a happy mistake, whatever you want to call it." Jinn shrugged, recounting in his mind the day they were stolen. "He lost us, the vessels containing us were all taken. In retrospect, you'd think he would have been more careful, but I think the power got to his head. He thought he was untouchable. It was through a series of thieving, bargaining, and bribery that we all went our separate ways. For me, it was decades before someone realized I was inside the vessel. There was nothing we could do about it. It seems he has created more, or at least found a way to trap others that were already out there."

"You're saying he doesn't honor his deals?" Briar asked.

"Unless he has turned a new leaf, which I highly doubt, no, he doesn't," Rosie muttered, and rolled her eyes which told Jinn that she was ready for the conversation to be over. She, like anyone else who knew the warlock, hated the reminder of her creator. He knew that it was all she could do to not think of the man who stole her happy life away from her.

"Sucks for Cast, but we have to stop this guy. Something tells me that once he takes out your people, he isn't going to stop there." Jax was reconsidering his position of hands off. If the warlock in question had created beings of such powerful magic, there was no telling what he would do. It meant that the dragons wouldn't be safe from him. No one would be.

"Looks like we're in this together." Briar smiled at the man she hoped to someday be able to call her friend again.

"Just like old times, huh? Guess I should introduce the team." He turned to the squad of men standing behind him. With each introduction, the man whose name he called stepped forward. "Here we have five of the best we have to offer you. Joe is a great strategist, Rick is a fighter, strong and fearless. Brandon is quick, the fastest we've got. The twins, Marcus and Maximus, are like nothing you've ever seen before."

"You give us your best?" Briar questioned. She'd expected a

standard escort, not the elite lineup he'd introduced.

"Well, you're a powerful entity yourself. We need someone who can keep up with you." He winked, and she caught his meaning. The dragons didn't trust them. The men were the best because only their best had a chance of taking down the fairy queen should she step out of line. "I will meet up with you all later, I know the route you're taking. Unfortunately, there is only one open path that will allow access to Cast's island. I will meet you before you enter."

"Great, a journey through dragon land, and on foot. This should be fun," Praia muttered, catching the eye of Rick who smiled.

"You'll be safe." He winked at the fae girl before catching Joe's elbow to his side.

"All right then, let's get a move on, shall we?" Rosie sauntered forward, eyeing the dragon men. "I would really like to hurry up and get back to my penguin babies."

"Did she say penguin babies?" Briar looked to Jinn who laughed and shook his head.

"Don't ask."

"This place is gorgeous." Praia spoke softly as they walked on. She'd been to the lands once before the dragons claimed it as their own. Her memories in no way did the place justice. Again, the group was pushed to the edges of the country, traveling by foot through what was once known as Gippsland Lake Coastal Park. Once a little human community, the area had been returned to nature. Rising seas washed away all evidence of its former inhabitants. The dragons were eager to let the area return to the sea—it meant there would be plentiful fishing grounds and a reinforced barrier land. Still there was enough land left to make the trek that would take them to the former island of Tasmania where Cast was being held. Even in its swamp like state, Praia reveled in the beauty of it all. Her enhanced senses gave her access to sights the others may not have been privy to.

"It gets even better, you know." The flirtatious dragon, Rick, moved closer to her. "This is just a small taste of what the Cascades has to offer."

"Is that so?" She couldn't help herself. The man was gorgeous, with smooth ivory skin, eyes that lit up like stars, and a smile that could shatter the sun. It wasn't often Praia got a chance to be near a man without scrutiny, so she had to flirt with him, especially with the way he was looking her over.

"Yes, perhaps someday I can give you a full tour." He winked at her, flashing that stellar smile again. "What do you say I take you for a flight? You can climb on my back, I'll carry you."

"Keep it in your pants, Rick," the dragon described as a nerd said. Joe was usually left with the task of keeping the wayward dragon in check. Rick had promised so many women a midnight ride in the sky, in exchange for a roll in the hay.

"Oh, let the boy flirt a bit, no harm in it." Rosie popped over to Joe's side. Her finger ran along the flesh of his muscled arm. "At least, none that I've ever found."

"Here we go," Bruto muttered, catching a hard side eye from Rosie.

Jinn smacked him on the shoulder. "Let it go, old man." Someday the two of them would stop denying the real reason they were always at each other's throats. Jinn, however, wouldn't be the one to point it out. That would be the day hell froze over and the sky above opened to swallow them whole.

"Yeah, yeah." Bruto shrugged. "Let's get this over with so I can get back to my ice cap."

"So, Joe, I assume you're the head of this group?" Briar addressed the supposed group leader. She knew that when it came to dragons, the most important was always introduced first as a show of respect to their status.

"You assume correctly." He smiled and gave a respectful bow to the queen, though she was not his own.

"Good. Tell me, what is the plan?" They walked on, but nothing more had been told of their intent. Briar had hoped the dragons would think to explain themselves, but when it became clear that they would not, she had to speak up.

"It's about a day's walk. We will do about three quarters of it today, stopping for a rest in a boarding home which we use for guests who may not be well received in the general population." He peered over his shoulder at the collection of beings following them. Not many of them would be welcomed with open arms ... well, possibly the bear. His people had a weird affection for bears. "It is fully stocked with what we need. There we will gather our strength, spend the night, and get back at it first thing. Jax will meet us on the path to Cast's island. He is needed to open the passage."

"He is? Why?" Mysti asked the question. Since they touched down, she hadn't moved far from Briar's side. Every move she made was closely shadowed by her second.

"What keeps Cast trapped on that island is blood magic. The blood of the king was used to seal it. Because of that, only he or one of the royal family can open the gates."

"Understood," Briar answered. Jax would in fact be joining them. She thought he might sit things out, but if he was the key to the door, she could count on him being there.

"Wait, did he say that we aren't going directly there? We can't lose another night," Praia chimed in, she pulled her eyes and her thoughts away from the hunk at her side for a moment to join the conversation being held. "We can't wait another day! The eclipse is tomorrow!"

"We will get there in plenty of time, during the day when they will least be expecting an attack," Brandon, a wisp of a man with a mop of brown curls on his head, who'd remained silent since his arrival, spoke up. He needed to squash any concern that Praia may have brought up in the group. Rumbles of worry were already spreading, and as the man usually tasked as pacifier, he couldn't allow the group to get riled up.

"Briar, you have to see that this is a mistake. We can't keep waiting, the clock is ticking," Praia spoke up again, ignoring the reassurances offered. There was much more on the line for them than anyone else, the urgency wasn't the same.

"I agree," Mike offered. Praia's anxiety was contagious, and the members of his group were already beginning to stir because of it. If the eclipse happened before they made it to Daegal, they were screwed, and every person with him understood what that meant. "The closer we get to that eclipse, the weaker you all become, and the less likely it is that my people get out of here okay."

"Even if I do agree with you all, this is not our land. Like it or not, we have to play by their rules. If we work effectively, tomorrow we will get to Daegal in time enough to stop his plan," the fairy queen stated with a confidence and surety that was more than anything a mask to hide her mirroring concerns.

Jinn pulled Briar to the side. "Are you sure about this?" Out of respect for her new status, he let her call the shots. It was necessary for the end goal: peace. However, there was an undeniable flaw facing them—if they failed, it would mean Daegal would succeed and Nitara's life would be at stake. He wanted peace, but not at the expense of her life.

"Not at all, but really, what am I going to do?" She was stuck in another territory, and she couldn't throw her weight around. Besides, she was a new queen, not established at all. "You have any other ideas that don't end with us getting chased down by a bunch of fire breathing dragons?"

"Unfortunately, no I don't." He looked over his shoulder at their escorts. "I don't like this."

"Well, I suppose we will have to go along with their plan." She paused, thinking. "You think you can reach Nitara again? Maybe get a message to her or gather some more intel as to where he is in his plans?"

"I've tried, trust me, I have. There is something blocking me. I think Daegal may have realized I reached out to her, I'm not sure how." Twice he attempted to reach her, to hear her voice again and reassure her that he was coming to save her. Each time he hit a hard block that refused him access to her. She was still there, but the connection was being scrambled, interrupted somehow.

"Shit. Well, I guess we're going in blind."

"Looks like it."

CHAPTER
TWENTY
THREE

The walk wasn't very eventful. Besides a stray animal here and there, they ran into no other living beings. From time to time, off in the distance they would see dragons taking flight in the sky. Brandon told them it wasn't common to have so much air traffic. He assumed the locals were just trying to get a sight of the odd collection of beings there on a common mission. Mike wasn't the only one looking to broker peace. To see them together, meant that there was hope for change. There were others, however, who wanted to see them fail and took to the sky hoping to get a view of the moment when it happened.

As they progressed, the group remained segregated—very few

mingled outside of their own. Mike's people remained by his side, bringing up the rear of the group. Rosie mixed and mingled, but Bruto kept to himself on the outskirts of the group as if preparing for a quick and easy exit should things get hairy. The fae and fairies, though similar in many ways, shot questioning glances across the path. Praia, often fielding questions about the new queen, tried her best to launch her own inquiries about the dragons. It wasn't often she was able to be around them, and despite the dislike between their kind, she was always very curious about them. Though it was Rick who answered most of her questions, the twins, Marc and Max, chimed in from time to time, filling in gaps in the information. She was surprised by how open they were but accepted their gift of knowledge happily.

"Here is where we will stay for the night," Joe announced, pointing ahead to the three brown buildings that stood out like a sore spot in the area before them. There were no other structures, these three having been rebuilt after the human town was washed away. As he said, it was a guest facility.

"About time," Mike huffed. "Remind me again why we are walking when all of you have magic that can transport us?"

"A show of respect." Briar shook her head, laughing at the expression on his face. For a king, Mike was horribly out of shape and every excursion they went on further proved that he needed to hit the gym.

"Right, right. Respect." He stomped forward, muttering how the dragons could have respected them by giving them a ride to the damn place.

The buildings looked more like office space than a place for rooming. Though there were beds, food, and water, that was pretty much it in the way of accommodations. No one complained. The spaces were quickly divided up—again, people staying with their own. The centermost building was where Jinn, Praia, Mike, and Briar held up with the dragons.

"I hope you don't think I will be sleeping here." Rosie pointed to the bed and shot Bruto an abhorred look as if he had chosen the accommodations himself. "Look how hard this mattress is. I'm not about to ruin my fragile figure sleeping on a thing like that!"

"Oh hush, woman. It's one night!" Bruto commented, ridiculing the woman who scrunched up her nose, indicating the sheet she lifted from the bed had a foul smell.

"I will do no such thing. If you want to sleep like a peasant, feel free. I will not." She dropped the fabric to the floor, turned, and exited the room.

"Where are you going?" Against his better judgement, Bruto followed Rosie out of the room and into the hall.

"To create something more comfortable for myself, obviously."

"You can't do that, Rosie," he warned. "You heard what Briar said, we are in their land, we need to respect their customs."

"You want me to be concerned with who, the dragons? If they are so concerned about me creating a little plush nest for myself, they have to seriously reevaluate their priorities." She huffed and continued on her way. "I will not charge into battle after sleeping on that brick of a mattress under sheets that hold the stench of animal urine!"

She climbed the stairs to the top floor. Reaching above her head, she pointed her finger at her chosen spot on the ceiling. The material above her cracked and turned to dust as an opening appeared. From above, a staircase carpeted in pink and paired with a gold banister fell to her feet. She clapped her hands, giddy to enjoy her creation. Bruto followed the woman up the stairs to the luxury bedroom she'd made.

"Damn, this is a lot more than just a comfortable place to sleep." Bruto scanned the room. With high ceilings, and large paned windows, the space was triple the size of the room she'd been given. Plush cushions lined the walls, just as they had in her home. At the back was a large vanity and closet filled with clothing she would never have a chance to wear. In the center of the room, draped in lilac and fuchsia silks was a large round bed. The place was a getaway, nothing meant for an overnight stay.

"Well, hell, tomorrow could very well be our last day in the land of the living. Shouldn't we enjoy our final night?" She twirled around the room before falling in the bed.

"I supposed we should." He laughed at her as she pulled herself back to her feet, the plush bedding making the task more daunting than expected.

"See, you agree with me." She walked over to him, swaying her hips in a familiar way that always led to Bruto saying something inappropriate and ended with him receiving a firm hand across the face. Realizing the trap, she was setting, he backed away and headed for the exit.

"I'm going to go see what they got for grub. Will be nice to have something I didn't have to conjure, you know." He laughed nervously and bolted down the stairs.

Rosie giggled at the man; as large as he was, he was still afraid of her. Rosie always took pleasure in knowing the effect she had on Bruto. She peered out the window and stared up at the sky, watching dragons fly off in the distance.

As the sun began to set, the atmosphere calmed. Dinner was served, outside under the darkening skies, a feast fitting their objective. They were going into battle and they needed fuel. Mike's men, having never enjoyed such a delicious meal freely, stuffed their plates and their stomachs with succulent meats, warm breads, and pasta with cream. The dessert tray was quickly cleaned of its puffs and pastries. There was plenty to go around. The dragons had prepared the meal for them as instructed by their king. They were guests and he would not have word get out that he hadn't shown them the absolute best hospitality.

"Thank you for this." Jinn nodded to Joe as he watched the

others eat. For a moment it seemed they were actually getting along, their preconceptions of one another fading. Good food had a way of bringing people together. "You didn't have to prepare such a meal."

"We dragons never go into battle on an empty stomach. You'll need energy if what you say is true, and we burn a lot of energy."

"I'm sure you do." Breathing fire had to be a major calorie burner. "So, Jax will be meeting us tomorrow?"

"Yes, with others as well. We are merely the escort party." Joe nodded at a fae woman who walked by, flashing a wide smile his way.

"I think you're more than that, but either way, we are appreciative of your efforts in all of this." Their conversation was cut short, interrupted by the sound of music and laughter in the background. They turned to see Bruto, hands full of food, dancing to his magically produced music. The upbeat tempo wasn't his usual operatic choice, but the bottle of beer in his left hand had put him in a different mood. The music helped to further lighten the atmosphere and ease the tension between the species there. Both fae and fairy joined in on the dancing, neither ever able to ignore a good song. The shifters laughed and watched as the drunken djinn was overtaken by the magical cousins and pushed off the dance floor.

As the party continued, Jinn found Briar. She sat at a table in the grass, surrounded by her guards, Mysti right at her side as always. "A word?" he asked.

She nodded to her companions—she didn't want them to follow

her. Leaving the table, she walked with Jinn and watched the dancing as she did. It was hard, even for her to ignore the urge to dance.

"I have a bad feeling about Joe." Jinn followed her line of sight.

"You too?" She turned to walk in the opposite direction of the subject of their conversation. Her gut told her that something with the guy wasn't right. She'd been keeping a close eye on him. So far, he hadn't done anything out of the ordinary, but she still didn't trust him.

"Something doesn't sit well. He seems familiar." He shook his head. "I can't place what it is."

"Familiar, in what way? Have you met him before?" She looked over her shoulder to the dragon who now stood with one of his own, scanning the party with his eyes.

"No, I've never laid eyes on the man, I definitely would have remembered him." He leaned in, lowering his voice even more, afraid of being overheard not only by the dragon, but any other one of the creatures with advanced senses. "It's more along the lines of how Bruto and Rosie were familiar to me before I ever knew them, it's something that ties us together."

"Something that ties you together?" His words tumbled around her mind, pieces of a puzzle slowly forming to make one disturbing picture. "You don't mean …"

"Yes, the magic that created us." Jinn found Joe again. The feeling was undeniable. Across the way, Bruto caught his gaze and gave him a knowing nod. Jinn wasn't the only one to pick up on the abnormality.

"You think he is in on this with Daegal?" Her guards still sat at the table where she left them, most of them relaxed, but Mysti had her eyes trained on the queen. Sensing her discomfort, she moved to come to her, but Briar lifted her hand and her eager guard remained where she was. If Joe noticed her running to the queen's side, it would do more harm than good. He couldn't know that they suspected him.

"I wouldn't put it past him, or anyone else." The djinn peered around the party in front of them, lingering momentarily on Mysti, a pause Briar hadn't caught. There was no magical familiarity there, but his gut still told him that something wasn't right with that woman. She never did anything to make him suspect her, but then again, neither had Joe.

"We need to let the others know, subtly." She touched his shoulder and smiled, keeping the appearance of two friends in casual conversation.

"Agreed." He returned a small smile and paired it with a low chuckle.

"Do you think Jax is aware?" What if her former friend was involved? Had he led them into a trap?

"No, I don't. If he was, the feeling would be there with him as well, but it isn't. I don't get it from any of the others, only Joe."

"Well, that's good. Only one traitor amongst us."

"Let's hope so. Let's hope he isn't planning to fuck over his own people as well as us." He grunted. "They already have one crazed dragon locked up. Who's to say he didn't spark some inspiration in the others? This could be a play for power. Hell, if Daegal is involved, that's definitely what it is. He loves promising power he can't or doesn't want to deliver."

"What if he is taking us in the wrong direction?"

"He isn't, I've been tracking our movement. I know this place well. Spent many years here once. Besides, the others don't know he is dirty. They would have spoken up if we were going the wrong way."

"I'm going to speak to Mysti and the others, they will get the word out into the group quietly. Can you take on Mike and your friends?"

"Bruto knows, and if he does, so does Rosie. I'll talk to Mike." Jinn stepped away from Briar and headed directly for the food, using the appearance of hunger as a misdirect for any suspicion that may have been raised by their hushed conversation. In addition, Briar's touch on his shoulder and soft whispers should inspire rumors of a budding romance. It wouldn't be something the fairies would approve of, and the djinns would be pissed if they believed it possible, but it was better for them if people suspected illicit behaviors. He kept his eyes away from Joe, focusing on his task of filling his plate and chatting with whoever came near. Not too much, though, as that too may cause suspicion as he hadn't been too quick to converse with anyone the entire time they'd been in the Cascades.

Briar had just stepped away from Mysti, who took to the shadows;

she used the cover to hide her urgency. Standing alone, behind the building she was meant to sleep in, she stared up at the sky. Nothing was going right, and she wished that she could have Alesea there to guide her. Staring at the moon, she said a small prayer for her lost friend before the moon was blocked out by giant wings.

"What the hell are you guys doing here? Just relaxing?" The dragon landed on the ground, his body returning to its human state.

"Jax?" Briar met the man as he stepped forward. "What are you doing here?"

"Yes, I guess you would be surprised to see me here, interrupting your festivities," he fumed. "Hell, I didn't know you all came here for a vacation."

"We didn't." She rolled her eyes, irritated by his attitude. "We're following your directives."

"Mine?" Jax stepped forward. "My orders were not for you to bunker down here and party. I thought you all had a war to fight!"

"Joe spelled it out for us. We were to rest here and move tomorrow morning." Briar kept an even tone. Though she was frustrated with the dragon, she would not show any disrespect in his home.

"That was not the directives he was given." Jax scouted the area. "Fuck, I had a feeling about him. I hoped I was wrong."

"Excuse me?" she whispered angrily, etiquette out the window. "You knew he was in with Daegal and yet you still sent him with us?"

"You know?"

"Yeah, we figured something was a little off with the dragon you left in command."

"Fuck, well, we need to get moving. We should strike tonight, waiting another day is too risky. I'm surprised you agreed to this," he snapped at her.

"I was trying to be respectful," she bit back.

"What?" He stared at her. "Don't tell me you're changing on me now that you have that pretty crown to sit on your head."

"What does that mean?"

"It means, the Briar I once knew would have never accepted such a foolish plan. She would have put her foot down and demanded that you kept moving." He dressed quickly in a pair of pants he pulled from a sack on his side. "Now, you're just doing whatever you're told? No questions asked?"

"It's different now."

"Why?"

"Because I represent all of my people. I can't just go around stomping my foot to get what I want."

"Perhaps not, but you also can't just accept whatever dumb ass plan is thrown at you when you know damn well that there is a better way. That is why we're in the mess we're in now. No one wants to stand up and say something, everyone just accepting shit that they know isn't right." He started off toward the party. It was time to light a fire under their guests' asses.

"Did you come here to lecture me on how to be a better queen?"

"No, I came here to warn you, but it looks like I'm too late." He looked up to the sky. Where the moon had once stood alone, the sun was reemerging to share the space.

"What the hell?" She blanched as she saw what he had.

"It's the eclipse!" He grunted.

"How? This isn't supposed to happen until tomorrow." She followed him.

As they entered the area where the others were gathered, the music stopped. All eyes were glued to the sky.

"Well, it seems our unwanted friend found a way to move up the timeline on that. We need to move, and now!"

"Sir, Joe is gone!" A burly dragon, one new to the group, ran up, alerting Jax that the traitor had escaped.

"We'll deal with him later. Gather the others and get everyone in the yard. We have to get to the island now."

"What the hell is going on?" Mike approached, directing his question to Briar.

"Daegal is fucking up the plan is what. We gotta move. Get the djinns and anyone else with the ability to transport."

"The no magic ban has dropped," Jax added. "We need to get every one of you out of here and to that fucking island. Immediately."

Briar looked up to the sky. "If we don't move now, we're all screwed."

Following the orders of the new queen, Mike sent his men to alert Jinn and the fairies. Having seen Rosie slip into the building, he took it upon himself to tell her. He climbed the stairs to the plush room she'd constructed above the brown structure.

"Yo, we gotta get going!" He ran into the room and instantly stopped and turned his back on the scene in front of him. "Oh, shit, sorry."

"Man, you never heard of knocking?" Bruto pulled up his pants, covering the muscled ass that had just greeted Mike.

Rosie laughed at them both. "Aw, Brut, don't be so upset. It was a simple mistake." She stood from the plush bed. "How can we help you, Mike?"

"Well, clearly you haven't heard the chaos downstairs. Our timeline has been moved up. Daegal is making his play now. We have to get going."

"What?" Bruto huffed as he struggled with the button on his pants.

"Look out the window." Mike pointed without turning around.

The large, ginger-haired man peered out the lace covered frame at the sky. "Shit, how is he doing that?"

"Your guess is as good as mine, but we need to get going. Everyone is rounding up downstairs, if you two care to join us."

"Absolutely." Rosie waved her hand and the frilly dress she sported disappeared, replaced by combat wear. "How 'bout it boys? Ready to stir up a little hell?" She waved her hand again and disappeared from the room.

"She's a handful, isn't she?" Mike finally turned to Bruto who looked a bit less disheveled. Now that he wasn't exposed, he was able to calm down.

"Man, you have no idea." Bruto put his shirt back on. "Let's get going, shall we?"

Outside, the members of their group were all collected. Jax stood at the head with Jinn and Briar at his side. Joe, of course, was nowhere to be found, but the bounty had already been placed on his head. Jax would be sure that he didn't get off with a shitty sentencing. He wouldn't be held captive; he would pay for his betrayal.

"All right, as you all can see, we don't have much time to get this done. We aren't far from the entrance. Those who can fly, take to the skies. Those who can't, one of our magically inclined friends will transport you. Considering what is happening here, I say we are in for a battle like nothing else I've seen before. Keep your heads down, stay alert. We don't know what he has going on in there or who he has with him. We've been monitoring activity, and after years of nothing, the island has suddenly burst into action. There are about twenty others there. We know at least a handful are witches, and some the captured djinn, the others are wild cards. Dragons are joining this fight, with full force." As he spoke, above his head, the shadowed figures of dragons moved across the sky headed in the direction of Daegal's hold out.

Jinn stepped forward. "Bruto, you will go ahead, do some recon on the area. Don't get too close, he will be able to sense you. Rosie, assist with the transport." Bruto nodded and disappeared while Rosie gathered up her group. Fairies and fae alike took to the sky, a few remaining behind to help with transporting the shifters who couldn't fly. They were able to use their affinity for air to lift the groups and carry them to their destination.

"You ready for this?" Briar laid her hand on Jinn's shoulder, both knowing what he was risking. The closer he got to Daegal, the more chance there was that he would be affected by the warlock's magic.

"As ready as I will ever be." He turned to Jax. "You flying?"

"Nope, figured you could give us a lift." The dragon placed his hand on his free shoulder, and in a puff of blue smoke, the three disappeared, leaving the field empty.

CHAPTER
TWENTY
FOUR

They appeared on the side at the bridge that had been built between what was once Tasmania and Australia. The translucent structure was one of magic. Without the blood of a royal, they would never be able to cross. Jax was needed to make it a solid form. The island itself was protected by a forcefield that was supposed to stop anyone from entering or exiting. Clearly Daegal had found a way around it. Above, those with wings flew, scouting the area. On the ground, the shifters waited for instructions.

Jax stepped forward and gave a nod to those who surrounded him. "Are we ready for war?" he called out, and the dragons above roared. The shifters below howled, growled, and pummeled the ground. Every one of them was poised to take off as soon as given the go. Jax lifted his hand to the sky, and with one finger used a razor-like talon of his dragon and slit open the palm of his hand. Drops of his blood fell to the bridge, the magical key working to unlock the hidden barrier. The translucent structure turned solid, and Jax signaled for everyone to proceed. Those in the sky flew into the opening while those below ran forward.

As the beast charged forward, and dragons, fae, and fairies flew above, Jinn found his friends. Each of them could feel the pull of the magic that created them.

"You ready for this?" Bruto took a deep breath. "Shit, that is strong. Was it always like this?"

"Yes, it was." Rosie had lost all her pep. Feeling the man who she hated so much and knowing how much he still could control her, filled her with an all too familiar anger. "What's the plan, Jinn?"

"If we can feel him, he damn sure can feel us. You two head for the boundary. Take as much of his attention from me as you can, but don't let him in your head. Once he is in there, he has you."

"You don't mean to tell me you're going in there?" Rosie questioned. "Not by yourself."

"Yeah, I am. What choice do I have?" He smiled at her. "I won't be by myself. We have a lot of help in there."

"You're crazy man. The second you do, he's got you," Bruto spoke up. "At least let me go with you, we can work together."

"No, it has to be this way. If we are all there, we have no way of breaking his focus. If I'm in trouble, I'll signal you both and you can come running to the rescue." He sighed and hugged Rosie who looked ready to cry. "What else would you have me do? Nitara is in there and we don't have much time before the eclipse is complete."

"I don't like this plan at all." Rosie waved her hands in the air but caught the stern expression Jinn had on his face. She wouldn't be able to talk him out of it. "Be careful. Okay?"

"Aren't I always?" Jinn asked.

"No!" both of his friends responded in unison and they all laughed.

Charging forward, Briar moved with her guards at her side. Jax had taken to the sky to join the other dragons while she remained closer to ground level, providing cover for the shifters who ran. The place was littered with magical landmines—explosions and traps that would have severely cut their numbers down if not for the fairies who shielded them from any injury.

The ground below them became shadowed as a massive dragon swooped down and turned to man before he landed.

"Redirect your people!" Jax shouted to them. "They aren't where we thought, they're at Freycinet!" Daegal, ever the strategist, had moved his headquarters to the peninsula. Knowing they would have shifters on their sides, people who couldn't fly, it meant cutting down their point of attacks. There was only one way in and out, and no doubt that path would be heavily guarded.

"You're going to have to give us a bit more direction than that." Briar responded.

"Head east until you hit water then south. It's not far from here. Hurry."

"You three, keep cover of the runners, the rest with me!" Briar headed for the peninsula. She was flying head first into a trap, but she had no choice. She hoped like hell that Praia was having better luck.

Having received the same intel given to Briar, Praia chose another tactic. Leaving the battle against the witches, she took her fae to the water. With magic they created masks that allowed them to breathe underwater. Once below the surface, they used the same air magic to propel them forward.

They dove deep enough to avoid being seen from above the surface as they headed for the peninsula. While his attention was on the fairies and shifters who headed straight for him, the dragons would hit from above and the fae from below. She questioned where Jinn was but had no time to find him and ask his plans. She rubbed the charm that hung around her neck, but he hadn't responded.

Regardless, she had to move ahead with the plan.

Below the water, their path was clear; besides, a few fish, it looked as if they would meet no resistance. That was until the piercing noise cut her eardrum. She looked back to see them closing in—sirens. Daegal's reach went far, even beneath the seas. She gave signal to the others; it was time to fight. The women approached them quickly, powerful tails working better than the magical propellers they had. There was no outrunning them, not on their own turf. Even if they could swim faster than the finned women who chased them, more of the sirens were ahead of them. Praia smiled. Finally she was going to get in on some of the action. She stopped swimming, and held her hands out to her sides, waiting for the opposition to get within a good range. The others did the same, creating a large circle with their backs to each other. When the sirens were nearly on top of the fae, they all slammed their hands together. A massive ripple shot out from their circle. The force turned the tables in their favor. While the sirens were tousled, the fae attacked.

Mike was having his own battle on land, taking out witches as fast as he could, while at the same time dodging landmines. He caught a glimpse of Jinn as he appeared on the far end of the field, snapped the necks of two witches and vanished again. Daegal had a lot more people on his team than they thought. There weren't just cauldron stirrers. There were shifters, slithers, and even fairies who had turned dark. There were corrupt people in every house. Mike didn't care who it was, if they came at him, he cut them down.

Above, Cast emerged from hiding, and it would take Jax and all his men to take the beast down. Daegal had brokered a deal with the ice dragon to give him more power, and he hadn't fallen short on that. Cast was at least five times the size of any of the other dragons in the sky, and quickly he killed three of the opposition. Their bodies fell from the sky, crashing into the ground, killing any poor soul unfortunate enough to be trapped beneath. He swooped down, breathing a trail of ice across the ground that Mike barely dodged, but his friend, another slither, wasn't so lucky.

Jax lead his people with strength. Flying beneath the large dragon, they unleashed their fire at his belly, taking his attention from the fight on the ground. Again, and again, they used his size against him. Once the thick skin had become worn from the fire, they attacked, using sharp talons and teeth to rip the beast apart. Their fight took them over the water as Jax herded Cast to the sea with strategic attacks. When he finally fell, his massive body slammed into the ocean. Still they attacked with fire, and talons ripping at his throat. They had to be sure the one who betrayed them would never rise again.

The collapse of Cast into the ocean disrupted the battle beneath the waters. Where Praia was cornered by sirens, her people fought as hard as they could, but they were simply outnumbered. When the oversized dragon fell into the waters, his massive form remained a dragon, no longer able to turn back to his human counterpart due to the dark magic used to turn him into the monster he was. His body trapped both sirens and fae and dragged them down to the depths. Praia, heartbroken to see so many of her own taken away, turned and continued the fight. Still, she was outnumbered, and for the first time, worried that she might not survive. A redheaded siren swam directly at her. She had a spear in hand. Praia looked for a way out, but she was blocked on all sides. She lifted her hand to rub the medallion charm around her neck, to say her final farewell to Jinn. Before she could get the message across, the siren who approached her was snapped in half. The massive jaws of a sea dragon broke her in half by biting down with razor-like teeth, ripping her apart. The remaining sirens tried to flee, but it was too late for them. The dragons made quick work of them before joining Praia on her swim to Freycinet.

CHAPTER
TWENTY
FIVE

When her head broke the surface of the water, Praia took in the sight on the shore. Jinn was in an all-out battle with Bruto! She gasped as they threw blows at each other. Bruto attacked Jinn, who merely dodged the assaults and only hit hard enough to deflect his friend. Praia started to swim toward them—she wanted to help Jinn, but the appearance of Rosie assured her that Jinn was not on his own.

"Bruto!" Rosie called out. "You have to resist; you have to fight this!" Fortunately, and what was surely the first time it had ever been an advantage, Rosie had so much unresolved anger in her heart for the one who created them, that she was able to use that hatred to block his influence over her. She could feel his pull, his attempt to get inside of her head. Each time his voice would register, giving her a familiar itch at the back of her brain, she would flash back to a life she once had, to the family, the child she was taken away from. That loss made her strong, strong enough to resist.

Jinn had also managed to avoid the hold of Daegal. He chose to focus on Nitara and the connection that still existed. The closer he got to her, the stronger that connection felt. He also felt Daegal trying to get in, but he resisted, because he had to.

Bruto was not as strong. Against his own will, he attacked Jinn relentlessly. Daegal wished it so, and Bruto had to do what he was asked. Rosie tried to take his attention from Jinn, but to no avail. As long as Bruto attacked, Jinn would be distracted and unable to save his wife and ruin the warlock's plans. As it was, there was no other immediate threat. The warlock, who she still hadn't seen, wasn't within sight. Though he influenced what was happening, he hadn't the balls to show up in person. The dragons still fought in the sky with creatures that Daegal had conjured from the shadows. The demons were cut down by fire, but the threat was boundless—the more they destroyed, the more he conjured.

Off in the distance fairies fought with witches as they tried to penetrate the narrow access point to the peninsula. Briar was trapped, her powers fading faster as the moon eclipsed the sun; Praia, though weakened, was still strong. Sitting in the water, watching it all play out, she had the most hope of saving them.

Aborting her plan to run to the shore, she searched for a better way of helping them and found it in the sky. The other djinns were still secured by the witches atop the peak of the hill. The sound of heavy wings cutting through the air announced Praia's chance to act. Using the same air magic that propelled her through the water, she shot from the sea and landed on the back of the dragon she recognized. It was time he gave her the ride he'd promised. "Take me to them!" She pointed to the trapped djinn when he looked at her. Rick turned his body and headed for the peak.

The eclipse was getting closer and she would only have one shot, her energy was already fading. If she could somehow stop the djinn, release them from whatever magic was containing them, perhaps they would be strong enough to resist Daegal, just as Rosie and Jinn were. When Rick got her close enough, she leapt from the dragon's back and fell to the ground in the center of the djinn. Six were in chains, pulled to their knees in a circle around two who were standing in the center. All their eyes were smoke filled. Whatever they were seeing, it wasn't Praia or the war around them.

Realizing there was no hope of gaining their attention, the fae pulled a knife from her back and quickly ran to the three witches that sat just outside of the circle, chanting. Her first victim felt the cold blade as it ran against her taught throat, ending her incantation with a gurgling sound. Praia moved quickly from the first to the next and drove her knife into the chest of the second witch, but before she could get to the third, the woman ran. Though the ritual had ended, and the spell was interrupted, the djinn continued their slow approach toward each other. She knew simply ending the spell wouldn't be enough, but it was a start.

In the hands of Nitara was the Lunaire stone, and the Solaris was held by another djinn, a man whose skin was the shade of fire. Both of their eyes were closed as they moved blindly forward. As they stepped closer together, they pulled the corresponding celestial object with them. Her first attempt was a foolish one in which she tried to rip the stone from the hands of Nitara, hoping the moon stone would recognize her as the child of its source of power, and come easily. It didn't. It was as if the stone was fused to its new owner and neither budged no matter her effort. She tried to use air to push them apart, but the effort did nothing more than give her a migraine. Frustrated and dizzied, she stopped.

"Shit!" she cried out. She had to try something else. Staring down from the peak, she witnessed Jinn as he continued his fight with Bruto, and Rosie who continued her attempts to intervene without hurting their friend. In the distance, Briar and her fairies were failing, the witches gaining more ground in the fight. Briar was restrained and forced to watch two fairies lose their lives as they tried desperately to defend their queen. So many lives had been lost, and if Praia didn't act, more would fall. In a last-ditch attempt to change what was happening, she forced all her strength into one final move. The concentrated current of air shot from her hand, creating a lasso that wrapped around the male djinn, from the other hand, another current wrapped around a boulder perched just at the edge of the cliff. With one final peer over her shoulder at her struggling friends, she ran and leapt off the cliff, using the remaining strength to shake the earth, knocking the boulder over the edge. The weight of her fall pulled the djinn with her and the two fell to the depths. Before she crashed through the surface, she witnessed Jax snatch Nitara from the fall. The magic had pulled her right along with them. As Jax flew away with Nitara as his haul, the stones were separated, and the sun and moon withdrew. Praia closed her eyes as her back crashed into the water, and she was dragged deep beneath the surface.

$$\partial J \partial$$

Briar felt the return of her power. Looking above, she saw that the sun and the moon were retreating, and with each moment that passed, she became more fueled by the reappearing sun. Kelli and Jani were dead—their bodies lay on the ground before her, and the witches responsible cackled as they prepared another assault. This time, Mysti was in their sights. She would be damned if they killed her second. Her wrists were bound by the vines of a nearby tree. The witch in red commanded them to obey her, but unfortunately, she like the others were already celebrating a victory they had not yet secured.

Briar called to her fire, and though the response was a weak one, it was enough to burn through the restraints that held her. Without her magic at its full strength, she had to use the combat training she'd done for years. She ran across the field, dodging fireballs launched from the dragons above who were on Daegal's side. As she ran, she lifted an abandoned sword from the ground. Raising it above her head, she landed the blade square into the neck of the woman in red, removing her head from her torso. With her death, the forestry withdrew their bindings and her fairies were freed. Back on even ground, they fought their adversaries, their battle cries echoing into the sky where the dragons continued to cut down their own set of traitors.

Large, winged bodies crashed to the ground, but Jinn kept his focus on Bruto ... until he saw her, in the clutches of a dragon, being flown away. The moment was all it took for Bruto to slip away from Rosie and land a blow to his jaw that took Jinn off his feet.

"Bruto, no!" Rosie cried.

Jinn looked up to see the burly redhead standing over him. Fear and sadness intermingled in his eyes and he stared down on his friend. "I'm sorry." Bruto lifted his hand, summoning his energy that glowed around his fist in an orange haze. Jinn prepared to defend himself, knowing it would mean the loss of one of their lives, but he could no longer avoid it. His own hand took on a blue glow at his side. Before either could draw fire, the arms of Rosie wrapped around Bruto and they vanished in a puff of pink smoke.

With the two of them gone, Jinn turned his focus to Nitara and the dragon who held her. No matter how much he searched, the sky was too active to make sense of things. Dragons fought along with other winged beings and there was no sight of her.

"Jinn!" Mike approached him, clothes torn, and body scarred. "Nitara, Daegal has her!"

"What?" Jinn yelled before he could contain his anger.

"Those damn dragons, they attacked Jax and took her!" Mike looked up. "Fucking traitors everywhere!"

"Where did they go?" Jinn demanded.

"I don't know, man. I'm sorry. She was there one moment and gone the next."

"Fuck!" He scanned the area; in the distance Briar still fought. "Where is Praia?"

"I don't know. I haven't seen her since she leapt in the ocean with the other fae." Mike scanned the shoreline. "She should have been here by now."

Jinn rubbed the medallion around his neck, hoping to connect to the fae girl, but there was no response. "Shit. Mike, I need you to find her!"

"What are you going to do?" Mike questioned the man whose hand still glowed in a blue aura.

"I'm going to find my wife." He reached into his pocket, pulling out the small stone carved in the shape of the crescent moon. He held it in his hand, using it to connect to her, to the woman who held his heart. As it warmed in his palm, spreading the heat throughout him, he knew it had worked. He closed his eyes and left behind the ensuing battle.

CHAPTER
TWENTY
SIX

"**L**et her go!" Jinn's voice reverberated around them, disturbing the wildlife in the trees of the thick forest. Birds flew from their homes, escaping the catastrophe that they sensed was about to happen.

"Ah, Jinn, finally you join us." Daegal spoke in the same sickly tenor that always coated his words. Time hadn't changed much about the man. "All these years, I've searched so hard to find you. Where were you?"

"Let her go, Daegal," Jinn repeated his demand, ignoring the attempt at distracting conversation.

"It was supposed to be you up there with her. She the moon,

you her sun, forever repelling one another, but for just a moment, coming together. It was to be your love story!" He shook his head, revealing the pale skin behind the dark hood that covered his face. The man may have been immortal, but the years had not been good to him. His skin was grey and translucent, his eyes a sickly yellow and his mouth black with rot. "Too bad, I guess this is just as good a way for the two of you to come to an end. I suppose I'll have to figure out my world domination another way."

"Nitara, are you okay?" Jinn asked the woman whose throat was wrapped in the long, gray fingers of the warlock.

"Jinn, you shouldn't have come here." Sorrow filled her voice. For the first time since he'd known her, the woman was without hope.

"You knew that I would. I could never leave you." Jinn stepped forward but Daegal pulled back. "I could never sit back and allow this to happen."

"Ah, see, so touching!" Daegal threw Nitara to the ground. "You two were always my favorites, and at the same time, you bring me such heartache!"

Nitara tried to run to Jinn but Daegal lifted his hand. A shadow reached out, expanding to the shape of his palm, and smacked her to the ground. The shadows continued to operate under his command and forced her to remain with her face in the dirt. The same force that restrained Nitara, knocked her husband away as he tried to run to her. His back slammed into a tree hard enough to crack the wood and send it falling to the ground. Daegal's laughter filled his ears. He lifted his hand to cover his ears, and realized the stone was still in his grasp.

Again, he used the stone to connect with her. The same warmth spread beneath his touch, and instead of taking him physically to her, his mind reached out. Under the weight of the shadow, that refused his body movement, he spoke to her.

"*Nitara, I'm here.*" He was in her mind again.

"*Jinn, I don't wanna die here.*" Her voice was weak, she had nearly given up. He could hear it, she was tired, and she had every right to be.

"*You won't, I promise, but we have to work together.*"

"*What do you need me to do?*"

"*He said that you are the moon, and I am your sun. When we get together, powerful things can happen. We must fight this; we need to get to each other. We are strongest together. That is why he is determined to keep us apart!*"

"*How? I can't move.*" Her voice, though internal, trembled with fear.

"*Nitara, we are stronger than this. Our magic is no longer bound by him. You know it. Focus on your magic. Connect to your power and refuse him the same way you were before! How did you do it? In that cage where I found you, you were fighting against him. I need you to do the same thing now.*"

"*Jinn, I—*"

"Listen, remember when we first got married?" he coaxed her. He had to get through to her.

"Yes."

"Do you remember what you told me?"

"Yes."

"Say it, now."

"There is no love stronger than ours. The sun, the moon, the earth, and the stars, they wish to have a bond as strong as ours."

"Nitara, I meant every word I said to you. You will have my heart for as long as the sun rises to kiss the sky, and for an eternity after it fades. I will not leave here without you, and I refuse to let you give up on yourself!"

"Okay. We can do this, together."

"Always together, Nitty."

Allowing the love that fueled his fight to reach through to her, Jinn called to the fighter inside of his wife. The bond between them strengthened as Nitara regained her hope. Even though they weren't yet together, they were strong. Jinn whispered through their bond, *"Fire,"* and the forest was set ablaze in blue and purple flames cutting through the shadows and releasing them from their hold.

In a blur they ran to each other, slamming into a firm embrace. In one show of the power of their unity, Nitara's light mixed with Jinn's and created a blast that dispersed the remaining shadows and left Daegal with none of his minions to command. He called them to him but there was too much light, no shadow could form. The fire subsided, only burning the immediate area and leaving the rest of the forest unharmed.

Daegal shouted curses at the two, and realizing that he had no choice, he gave up on the shadows and charged the two. Even without his shadows at his command, he proved still to be a difficult adversary. His power wasn't his own, stolen from those he'd tricked over the years. He opened his mouth and breathed a stream of ice, courtesy of the dragon, Cast. The ground beneath Nitara's feet froze and she slipped, slamming her head against the ice.

Daegal, never one to miss an opportunity, moved again—this time with intent to kill. But Nitara had enough left in her that she grabbed hold of Jinn's hand, again increasing his power by the connection. Jinn faced Daegal and the blue flames emerge tipped in the purple of his wife's magic. He defended her, putting a protective circle around her body, and taking his maker head on. Daegal used the one gift that was naturally his and called to his connection to the Earth to shake the ground beneath Jinn. Expecting the move, Jinn simply lifted from the earth, floating above the chaos beneath.

"You will fall!" Daegal called out as he attacked again with stolen breaths of ice.

Jinn dodged the stream, but not entirely. He grunted as the shards of ice cut into the side of his torso. He would heal, there was no time to respond to the pain. Instead, he whipped lassos of flames at his attacker. Daegal escaped one, but the other wrapped around his legs, pulling them from beneath him, and the man fell forward. The rope tightened and spread, creating a net of flame that crept up the length of his body, covering him in flames and burning him. Daegal cried out as his skin melted away. He reached with his free hand, hoping to use his magic once more, but Jinn reacted quickly and sent more flames to further restrain him.

"It's time that this comes to an end." Jinn stood above the burning man and ebbed the flames back. The rope no longer blazed but retained a soft glow of heat.

"I created you! You would be nothing without me!" Daegal choked out. Though the flames had subsided, he still burned, he still suffered. Jinn wanted that to continue. He could never inflict enough pain on the man, no amount of torture could ever make up for what he had done to them and so many others.

"You took away the thing that mattered to me most!" Jinn screamed, his voice echoing in the hollow forest. "You stole my life away from me! I owe you nothing!"

"You owe me everything! I will not die here!" Daegal laughed. "You're too weak to kill, too sensible!" There was a time when his assessment of Jinn was correct. There was a time when the man who stood above him valued life over revenge. There was a time when Daegal would have had a fighting chance at surviving. This was not that time.

"That's where you're wrong. See, when you turned me, you stole something else." Jinn leaned in, and the flames flared again and stretched until they reached Daegal's throat. "My ability to give a fuck about anything other than what I want." With that, the ropes tightened, crushing the warlock, and cutting through his body. His decrepit figure was severed in an unfathomable number of pieces and then burned until there was nothing of him left on the ground but cold dark ash.

Back home, Jinn forgot about the rest of the world. He took his wife away from the devastation and left the fairies, fae, and slithers to clean up the resulting mess. That was never his concern. She was. Nitara. He stood over her, watching her as the sun once again left the sky, giving way to the moon she loved so much.

"Jinn?" She stretched in the bed, coming to her senses.

"You're awake, finally." He smiled around a grimace as he lifted from the seat near the window. His wound was healing, but he would be sore for a while.

"Yes. Is he …" She looked around the room, as if expecting Daegal to pop out of a corner and attack her again.

"He's dead. I made sure of it." He made it to her side where he sat next to her and pushed stray hairs from her face. "You don't have to worry about him."

"I don't know how I could ever thank you." She smiled at him, and for the first time since he saw her locked away in the cage, a prisoner to a lunatic, she relaxed.

"You don't have to thank me for anything, Nitty. If it weren't for me, you wouldn't have been in this mess."

"You can't keep blaming yourself." She shook her head. "I could have left you when I realized just how foolish you could be." The small sound of her laugh warmed his heart.

His soft chuckle responded to hers. "I'm glad you didn't."

"So am I."

He leaned in, ready to plant a kiss on the full lips he'd missed for centuries, but she pulled away from him.

"Jinn," she pushed back further, "I'm sorry, I can't."

"What?" He straightened, giving her space. Had he done something wrong? Was she hurt?

"I'm so grateful that you came, and that you saved me, but I can't be with you." Large eyes teared as she spoke the words she hoped she would never have to speak.

"What are you saying? What do you mean you can't be with me?"

"It's been a long time without you. And for so long, I held on to the hope that you would come back, that you would take me away from all of this."

"I'm here, Nitara." He grabbed her hands, pulling them into her own—his hope that the contact would make her understand. "That is what I'm doing now."

"Yes, but you're too late." She pulled her hands from his. "I'm sorry."

"Too late?" She couldn't mean what he thought, she couldn't possibly say the words.

"I'm with someone else now." Her words were explosions inside his head. Bombs that left a white noise in their wake that drowned out all other sound. "Someone else who I love very deeply. I cannot betray him in this way."

"Nitara, you can't be serious." The anger inside was only pushed back by the visage of her tears.

"I'm sorry, Jinn, but I am." She took the necklace from around her neck, the one he had replaced when they'd returned to his home and placed it in the palm of his hand.

Before he could speak, the room filled with purple smoke, and the woman he'd fought for, vanished from his bed. Jinn sat alone in silence, long enough for the sunlight to pass across the floor and give way to the moon. The crescent in his hand felt like it weighed as much as the one in the sky. She wasn't coming back to him. No matter how long he waited.

Jinn sat there clutching the wooden charm in his hand so long it left an impression on the palm of his hand. His eyes were red with pain, restlessness, and anger. The pounding at the front door finally became too much for him to ignore. Too agitated to walk,

Jinn allowed his smoke to transport him. The door swung open to reveal the tired face of Mike.

"What the hell do you want, Mike?" Jinn held the door in his hand, not allowing Mike access to come in.

"Look, I know you to are all cuddled up in a loving reunion, but we have some shit going down out here. Do you think Nitara-,"

"Nitara isn't here." Jinn cut him off and it pained him to say her name,

"What where is she?"

"How the hell should I know, Mike," he let the door go. "She's gone. She said she doesn't love me anymore and she left. Plain and simple."

"Look, I'm sorry man, that's messed up and we can drink our weight and talk about how shitty it is later, but like I said, we need your help out here. I-," Mike was once again cut off by the gruff voice of Jinn.

"Whatever it is, I'm sure you all can figure it out on your own. I honestly couldn't care less about what you all think I need to do." Jinn slammed the door in Mike's face. With his anger boiling to the top, he vanished from his home. Had he waited a moment longer, he would have heard Mike's cry.

"Praia! Jinn! Praia needs us!"

THE END

ENJOY THIS BOOK?
YOU CAN MAKE A BIG DIFFERENCE!

Reviews are the most powerful tools in my arsenal when it comes getting attention for my books. Much as I'd like to, I don't have the financial muscle of a New York publisher. I can't take out full page ads in the newspaper or put posters on the subway.

(Not yet, anyway).

But I do have something much more powerful and effective than that, and it's something that those publishers would kill to get their hands on.

A committed and loyal bunch of readers.

Honest reviews of my books help bring them to the attention of other readers.

If you've enjoyed this book I would be very grateful if you could spend just five minutes leaving a review (it can be as short as you like) on the book's Amazon page.

WANT FREE BOOKS?
GRAB JESSICA'S BESTSELLERS TODAY!

Building a relationship with my readers is the very best thing about writing. I occasionally send newsletters with details on new releases, special offers and other bits of news relating to the Caged Fantasies line up.

And if you sign up to the mailing list, I'll send you a free copy of my best-selling book to date, *Siren's Call*. And *The Fire Within*!

You can get both books, for free, by signing up at"
WWW.SUBSCRIBEPAGE.COM/G5K2A5

ABOUT THE AUTHOR

Jessica Cage is a bestselling author from Chicago. She often bleeds elements of her home town into her work. You can find out more about her and her signature Caged Fantasies at www.jessicacage. com. You can connect with Mark on Twitter at @writa_jlodi, on Facebook at www.facebook.com/jcageauthor and you should send him an email at jessica@jessicacage.com if the mood strikes you.

CPSIA information can be obtained
at www.ICGtesting.com
Printed in the USA
LVHW091616071020
668212LV00002B/232